# 1.

When Mio died, this was how I thought.

Whoever made our planet must have made another planet at the same time, somewhere in the universe.

That would be the planet where people go when they die.

The name of that planet is Archive.

"Archavie?" Yuji asked.

Nope. Archive.

"Archavie?"

Archive.

"Archa," he said, and thought a little, before adding "...vie?"

Whatever.

There, in a place like a giant library, very quiet, very clean, it is very orderly.

At any rate a big place, with a corridor going all the way through, so long you couldn't see the end.

That is where the people who have left our planet live, in peace.

Now that I think about it, that planet is like the inside of our hearts.


"What do you mean?" Yuji asked.

Don't you remember, when Mio died, the family all said it, didn't they? That she would be in your heart.

"Yeah."

So, that planet is the place where the people from all over the world who live in people's hearts all live together.

As long as someone is thinking of them, they can continue to live on that planet.

"And what if everybody forgets about them?"

Hmmm. Then they have to leave that planet.

Then it's really "Goodbye."


On their last night, all their friends get together, and they have a farewell party.

"Do they have cake?"

Yes, they have cake.

"Do they have *ikura*?"

Sure they do. (Salmon roe is a favorite of Yuji's.)

"And do they…"

They have everything. You don't have to worry.


"On that planet, is Jim Button there too?"

Why do you ask?

"I know Jim Button. Isn't that the same as him being in my heart?"

## Takuji Ichikawa

**TRANSLATED BY TERRY GALLAGHER**

VIZ MEDIA
SAN FRANCISCO

Published by
VIZ Media, LLC
295 Bay St.
San Francisco, CA 94133

www.viz.com

Ichikawa, Takuji, 1962-
 [Ima ai ni yukimasu. English]
 Be with you / Takuji Ichikawa ; translated by Terry Gallagher. -- 1st paperback ed.
   p. cm.
 ISBN-13: 978-1-4215-1393-5 (pbk.)
 ISBN-10: 1-4215-1393-5 (pbk.)
 I. Gallagher, Terry, 1956- II. Title.
 PL871.5.C55I4613 2006
 895.6'36--dc22

                          2007026103

Printed in the U.S.A.

First paperback edition, February 2008

# Be With You

Hmmm. (He was probably asking because we had just read *Jim Button and Luke the Engine Driver* the night before.) I think so, maybe.

"Then, what about Emma, is Emma there?"

Only people are there.

"Huh?" Yuji asked.

Jim Button is there, Momo is there.

Little Red Riding Hood is there, and of course Anne Frank is there. Hitler and Rudolf Hess are probably there too.

Aristotle is there, and Isaac Newton is there.

"What are they all doing?"

They are all just living quietly.

"Is that it?"

What do you mean, "Is that it?" Well, I bet they're all thinking about something.

"Thinking? About what?"

It might be something really difficult. It takes a long time, until they come up with an answer. So, even after they go to that other planet, they still have to think for a long time.

"Mom too?"

No, your mom is thinking about you.

"Really?"

Really.

That's why you won't ever forget about her either.

"I won't forget."

But you're so young. You only knew your mother for five years.

"Yeah."

So there's a lot of things I have to tell you.

About what kind of girl your mom was.

How she met me, how we got married.

How happy she was when you were born.

"Yeah."

I want you to remember.

If I'm going to meet your mom when it's my turn to go to that other planet, you'll have to remember always.

Do you understand?

"Huh?"

Oh, that's all right.

## 2.

"Are you all ready for school?"

"Huh?"

"Are you ready? Did you put on your name tag?"

"Huh?"

Why is he so deaf? He wasn't like this when Mio was here. I wonder if there's something psychologically wrong with him.

"It's time. Let's go."

Yuji was halfway back to dreamland, but I grasped his hand firmly and we left the apartment. At the bottom of the stairs, I handed him over to one of his older schoolmates waiting there. Walking alongside the other kid, a sixth-grader, Yuji looked like a preschooler. He was six, but he was small for his age. He looked like he had just forgotten to grow.

Seen from behind, his neck was as thin and white as a crane's. His hair sticking out of his yellow cap was the color of milky Darjeeling tea.

This hair, now like some English prince's, should change into thick, round curls in a few years.

That's what happened to me. That's what happens from all the chemicals your glands start to pump out when you hit puberty. When that happens, Yuji will get a lot bigger, bigger than I am. And he will meet a girl, who will look a lot like his mom, and they will fall in love, and if all goes well, someday they will create a copy with half his genes.

That's what people have done since the beginning of time (actually, that's what most living things have done), and it is the routine that will go on as long as this planet continues to spin.

I jumped on my old bicycle, which I keep at the bottom of the stairs, and headed for the law office where I work. It's only five minutes away. Vehicles and I don't get along well, so I am grateful the distance is short.

I have been working in this office for eight years now.

That is not at all a short time. I got married, had a child, and then my wife left this planet for another. Eight years is long enough for all that to happen.

After all that, I am now a twenty-nine-year-old father of a six-year-old son.

My boss makes things easier for me.

My boss was an old man even eight years ago, and he is still an old man, and he will probably stay an old man until he dies. I cannot imagine an office manager who is not an old man. I don't know his age exactly. He must be over eighty.

He has always reminded me of some St. Bernard dog with a little keg of booze hanging from his neck. What my boss has hanging from his neck is just his double chin though. But he is quiet and warm and his eyes always look sleepy, just like a St. Bernard's.

If a St. Bernard were sitting at the far desk instead of my boss, I might not even notice.

I had always been weak, but when Mio died I became even weaker. I started to lose even the strength it takes to breathe.

For a very long time, I couldn't do any work, which caused a lot of problems for my office. But my boss didn't look for anybody else, and he waited for me to get better. Even now, he lets me finish work and go home at four o'clock. I don't want to leave Yuji home alone for long, and the boss keeps that in mind. Of course, it means less pay, but I gain precious time that money couldn't buy.

I have heard that in other towns they have after-school programs, but here we don't have anything as thoughtful as that.

And that is why I am grateful I live so close to the office.

When I arrived at the office, I greeted Ms. Nagase, who was already there.

"Good morning," I said.

She greeted me as well.

"Good morning."

Ms. Nagase was already working at the law office when I got this job. She says she started there soon after finishing high school, so by now she must be twenty-six or so. She is a quiet and serious woman, with a quiet face becoming to that sort of interior life.

Sometimes I worry about her, and whether there is a place for her among females who are not shy about expressing themselves.

Someone might be holding her down with an elbow, or poking her with their foot, and at some point she'll just fall off the edge of the earth, won't she? This is what I wonder about her.

The boss hadn't arrived yet.

Recently, his arrival at the office had been growing later and later. I don't think it was because he was walking slower though.

For a while, then, it was just the two of us in the office. That is all. A suitable number, considering the volume of work there was to do.

I sat at my desk and looked over all the memos clipped to my clipboard. Things like "Bank 2 p.m." and "Get papers from client" and "Go to the regional legal affairs bureau," all written in a barely legible scrawl. Messages from the me of yesterday to the me of today.

My memory is terrible. So I make a habit of routinely writing down the things I am supposed to do.

This weakness of memory is one of the many unfortunate characteristics that are part of me, the sum total of which proves there was a serious flaw in the plans used to create me.

A single spot.

I think it must have been erased with White-Out, and then whatever else was written on that spot later with ballpoint pen just wouldn't stick. Of course, this is just a metaphor, but the reality is probably not much different.

At any rate, I don't know whether the writing was blurred or scratchy, or whether the writing underneath came through, but in my head, some very powerful chemicals are secreted haphazardly, with very random results. This makes me the kind of person who gets more excited than necessary, feels anxieties that are completely inappropriate to the situation, forgets things I should never forget, and becomes unable to forget things I would rather forget.

This is very inconvenient. It limits my activities, and it tires me out. I make a lot of mistakes at work, and people tend to underestimate me even more than they should.

In other words, people treat me like an idiot. But I don't try to make excuses and say it's all because of these chemicals in my head. It's a pain, people don't understand me, but based on the evidence they're actually right.

My boss is a very generous person. He doesn't let me go, he keeps letting me work here. Ms. Nagase keeps a close eye on my work without making a big deal about it.

I am very grateful.

I took care of some work in the office, packed some papers in my briefcase, and went out. I rode my bicycle to the regional legal affairs bureau.

I don't have a driver's license. I tried once, during my second year of college, but I was never able to get past the test for the temporary license.

That was only a few months after I first realized there was something wrong with my brain. There was a *Click!*, a switch flipped, a light went on, and the needle on some internal gauge maxed out. So when I went to get my driver's license, I was still in a thick fog of confusion. Maybe I should just be happy I got as far as the exam for the temporary license.

On that day, with the instructor beside me, I sat in the driver's seat, and my blood was saturated with those chemicals. I felt more anxious than necessary and unable to maintain sufficient focus. My anxiety was like a row of dominoes falling, getting bigger as they went, growing with incredible energy.

This may have been what we call an exponential increase. Its incredibleness was really incredible.

I get to a point where I feel like I'm going to die.
I really think I might die.

When I was around that age, I thought that dozens of times a day. Even now I sometimes think it a few times a day.

So I never took the test. The same thing happened twice again after that, and in the end, I forgot about getting a driver's license.

At noon I sit on a bench in a park, and I eat the *bento* box I made myself. I live a frugal life, but still I pare away at the things that are to be pared away.

Whenever I eat a lunch from a convenience store, I always get an upset stomach. Other people might be fine with them, but food additives can be a matter of life or death for me.

The sensors in my body are many times more sensitive than normal people's. I am extremely sensitive to changes in temperature, humidity, air pressure. For that reason, I wear a wristwatch that has a barometer in it, so I can be prepared in advance.

Typhoons can be really awful.

I really admire the toughness of ordinary people. Sometimes I think of myself as some insignificant vegetarian species on the verge of extinction.

Somewhere in the *Red List of Threatened Species*, my name is probably listed.

In the afternoon, I made the rounds of several clients, and then I went back to the office.

I make sure I have my memos with me. I mark the clients I have visited with an X, so I can see what's left to do. If I don't do this, I may end up going twice to the same client, or I find myself back at the office having passed another without stopping.

I handed Ms. Nagase the papers I received from clients. I took care of a few things around the office, and then my workday was over. The boss never appeared.

I said "Goodbye" to Ms. Nagase, and I was about to leave.

Ms. Nagase stopped me, saying, "You know…"

"What is it?"

She made a troubled frown and tugged at the collar and sleeves of her blouse a few times.

"Hmmm," she said. "Nothing."

"Well then." I thought for a second, and then I smiled and said, "Goodbye."

"Goodbye."

Back on the bike, I flew back to the apartment. Yuji was lying down, reading a book. I looked at the cover. It was Michael Ende's *Momo*.

"Can you read that?" I asked. Yuji turned to me and said, "Huh?"

"Can you read that book?" I asked again, and this time Yuji answered, "I can read it. A little."

"I'm going to go buy something for dinner."

I changed into a pullover and jeans, and I asked Yuji, "What do you want to eat tonight?"

"Curry rice."

We opened the door to our one-room apartment and went out. Going down the stairs, I said, "We ate curry rice the day before yesterday."

"But that's what I want to eat."

"Now that I think about it, I think we ate curry rice on Sunday too."

"So? It's what I feel like eating."

"It'll take time."

"I don't mind."

"Okay."

So we went to the shopping center by the train station, and we bought curry roux, onions, carrots, and potatoes. As we walked, I carried the plastic bag in my left hand, and with my right hand I held Yuji's hand. Yuji's hand is always a little damp.

Because I am the sort of person who worries more than I should, whenever we walk in the street I hold Yuji's hand and I don't let go. I say to him, "You have to watch out for cars. You have to be careful."

"Sure."

"Dozens of people die from car accidents every day."

"Really?"

"That's right. If the same number of people died from accidents on trains or planes every day, we would think something was terribly wrong, and they would get shut down."

"So, are people going to get rid of cars?"

"No. There will be more of them."

"Why?"

"I don't know."

"It's weird."

It sure is weird.

On the way home, we checked out Park No. 17. (I wonder how many parks there are in this town? I've seen No. 21.)

As always, Nombre-sensei and Pooh were in the park.

I don't know Nombre's real name. He got his nickname when he was young and still writing educational theory for elementary schools. The first time I heard this, I asked him, "Does Nombre refer to those little numbers at the bottom of the page, in novels and things like that?"

"That's right," he replied.

He is always shaking, like a little dog that got wet in the rain. He is quite old, and that might be the reason.

"Why is that your nickname?"

He shook his head a little. Or maybe he just shook a little.

"Hmmm, can't say for sure. It could be that the people who knew me were trying to say that my life is a blank. No matter how many pages you turn, there is nothing but one white page after another, like a book with just page numbers at the bottom."

"Really?" I asked. He stared into space with the teary, clouded eyes of the old.

"I lived my whole life for my younger sister."

Pooh, the scruffy dog at his feet, yawned.

(This dog too had a real name, but Yuji had stuck him with the nickname Pooh.)

This is Nombre's story:

"My younger sister and I were thirteen years apart. There was a brother between us, but after our parents died, one right after the other, he soon left home and set out on his own. Only my sister and I were left in the house.

"My sister's body had always been weak, since she was a small child, and the doctor's diagnosis at that time was that she would not live to see her fifteenth birthday."

What's a diagnosis? Yuji was asking beside me. I was having trouble coming up with the right way to explain, and I said, "It's just what you think it is."

I thought so, Yuji said, smiling.

There is no doubt in my mind he was imagining something completely different.

"When my brother left home, my sister was fourteen, and I was twenty-seven. I had decided my sister and I should stay together, and I would see her through to the end. I was at a good age, and there was a girl I was fond of. But I put my sister first, and myself after that; with this lecture I admonished my wavering heart. The truth was, my sister's treatment cost a lot of money. That is why, even if my fondness for a certain someone had blossomed into something more, we would never have been able to make a home together.

"In this way, the days and months flowed by with surprising speed.

"It was really fast. I thought there must be something peculiar about me. It was enough to make me think somebody really, really smart was stealing my time from me.

"At any rate, it was over before you knew it.

"What is certain is that there is nothing that needs to be written in my book. If on the first page you write down the day of a boring man, about whom there is absolutely nothing to say, and then on every other page you write, 'Ditto,' that's all there is to it.

"Can you believe that? That was my life for thirty years.

"My sister died at age forty-four. By then, I was just three years from my sixtieth birthday.

"One thing I can say, though, is that even my life has definitely not been a blank. Even the life of a boring man about whom there is nothing to say has something in it. It is not empty.

"They may have been small, but I have known joy, and other emotions. Every day I would finish my work and go home. I would tell my sister, who was waiting for me, about what had happened that day, and, what can I say, it was fun.

"And that is the story of my life.

"If I had lived a different life, I would be a different person sitting here. People cannot choose their lives."

Today as well, Nombre is living his own life.
Together with Pooh, his scruffy old dog.

Yuji scratched Pooh under his chin, and as always the dog let out the strangest sound—more of a faint vibration of air than an actual sound. But even that vibration had a certain crescendo and diminuendo.

If I had to write it down, it would look like this: "~?"

Nombre had told me before that Pooh's previous master had taken his voice from him surgically.

Even when the other dogs in the park greeted him with a "Woof!" Pooh was only able to respond, "~?" It didn't seem to bother Pooh any though.

"Curry for supper tonight?" Nombre asked me, eyeing the grocery bag.

"That's right. How about you?"

"This is what I'm having," he said, showing me a package of fried smelts in a plastic bag. "Day-old merchandise is half-price. That's a good thing."

He brought his nose to the bag, sniffed, closed his eyes and made a happy face.

"This too is a small happiness."

For some reason, seeing the happiness on Nombre's face made me sad.

I don't know why. Just sad, that's all.

Could it be because his happiness seemed so hard-bitten?

A person so close to the final chapter of his life should have a little more in his hands.

Could that be why?

Watching Yuji and Pooh bouncing around, Nombre and I sat on the bench and talked about all kinds of things. That was when I revealed to him the plan I had been secretly thinking about for some time.

"I'm going to write a book."

Nombre shifted his position, to get a little more distance, and he squinted at me, trying to get my entire body within his field of vision. He raised both of his hands and said, "Wonderful! That is truly splendid!"

"You really think so?"

"I do. Books nourish the heart. They are the lamps that light the darkness, the joy that can outshine love."

"It's not anything quite so extraordinary. I thought I would write the story of me and Mio, just so Yuji might be able to read it someday."

"Mmm. I think that would be terrific. She was a wonderful woman."

"Yes, she was."

Yuji had grabbed Pooh by the neck and was pretending to chew on his ear. Pooh was making an awful face and going, "~?, ~?"

"It may be because of some illness, but my memory has gotten terrible," I went on. "I think I have to write everything down before I forget it all. About me and her."

Nombre gave a little nod. "Forgetting is sad. I myself have forgotten many things. Memory is the ability to relive that instant. In your head."

As he said this, Nombre pointed to his head. His shaking fingertip looked as if he were trying to write some words on his temple.

"Losing a memory means you can't relive those days again. As if your life itself is slipping from between your fingers."

He nodded several times at his own words and went on.

"So, writing things down is a good thing, I think. I'm sure your book will be much more interesting than my own book."

At this point he quite artfully blinked his eye.

"The act of reeling in childhood memories sparked the novels that are considered the best literature of the twentieth century."

Finally, he stood up, slowly. It looked very painful, as if the earth's gravity had doubled just below his feet.

"Well, it's time to go home. A small happiness is waiting for me."

Nombre began to walk, taking small steps. Pooh noticed, went to his side, and followed him.

"Goodbye," I said.

With his back still turned toward me, Nombre raised his right hand, and went away.

"Goodbye, Pooh!" Yuji said.

Pooh stopped, looked back and said "~?" and then raced to catch up with his master.

Before falling asleep that night, I talked to Yuji about the planet Archive. I added plenty of details to give the planet substance. Every question Yuji asked added weight to the planet's existence.

"So, what shape is this planet?"

Through this question, the planet took on a silhouette. I took a pen, and a flyer from the newspaper, and I drew a picture of the planet.

Like this:

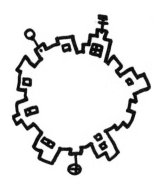

"The entire surface of the planet is taken up by buildings like libraries."

"No seas or mountains?"

"Nope. They took the tops off the mountains and used the dirt to fill up the rivers and the seas. Once they had gotten rid of all the ups and downs, they built buildings."

"Why?"

"Because there are an awful lot of people living on this planet. There's no space left over."

"Really?"

"Think about it. A lot of people are alive in my heart. They are all people who aren't on this earth anymore, but they all live on the planet Archive."

"Right. You already told me about that."

"If you took all the people living in the hearts of the people on Earth and added them up, how many would it be?"

"Hmmm. I don't know." (Think about it a little.)

"If every person has ten people living in their heart, that would mean over sixty billion people on the planet Archive." (Eliminating duplicates would decrease that number, but I'm not sure Yuji could understand that.)

"How many is sixty billion?"

"Well, in your school, you have about one thousand students in grades one through six. You see them all together at morning assembly, right?"

"I see them."

"Well, if you took your school and—wait a minute (counting zeroes on fingers)—multiplied it by sixty million, you'd have it."

"How many is sixty million?"

Admittedly, a good question.

"Hmmm, let me see. On top of the TV set, there's a plastic bottle with a lot of one-yen coins in it, right?"

"Yup. I've been collecting them for a long time."

"Well, I think there ought to be about one thousand one-yen coins in that bottle. So sixty million would be if we had all the coins in sixty thousand of those bottles."

"So...how many is sixty thousand?"

Still a good question.

"Well, let's see, sixty thousand. Hmmm. Well now—you and I go to the library a lot, right?"

"We do."

"I have heard that all the books in the library add up to about sixty thousand books."

"All the books in the library?"

"That's right."

"So that's sixty thousand..."

And then, for a long while, Yuji lay on the futon next to mine and thought about it. He was quiet for such a long time, I thought maybe he had fallen asleep. And then, in a small voice, he spoke to me: "Takkun?"

That's what he calls me.

"What is it?"

"Can I ask another question?"

"Sure."

"Well," he said. "What was the very first thing I asked?"

"Huh?"

"Yeah."

"Dad forgets too."

"Really?"

"Shall we go to sleep now?"

"Let's."

On a different night, Yuji asked, "Why did 'Somebody' create that planet?" And through that question, the planet Archive took on a reason for being.

"Well, I told you the buildings on that planet are like

libraries, right?"

"Yes, you did."

"So actually, that planet is a library."

"Really?"

"Really. The 'Somebody' who created the planet Archive really likes things like that. That's why the people who live on that planet write books for the 'Somebody.' Like I told you before, they're all thinking. Aristotle, and Isaac Newton, thinking about hard things, for a long time."

"Really?"

"Yeah. I told you Newton, and Plato, and everybody, had gone to Archive to think about the hard problems they couldn't solve on Earth, and that they are still thinking about them there—for hundreds and hundreds of years. As long as we remember them, they can continue to think."

"Okay."

"So, whenever they think of an answer, they write a book. And all those books are kept in the libraries of Archive."

"What about Mom's book?"

"Mom is writing a book too. She is writing about you and me."

"And does 'Somebody' read her book?"

"'Somebody' does. 'Somebody' particularly likes her book. Because it tells you about human love."

"Is that so?"

"It is."

"What does Jim Button write?"

"I think he probably writes books about trains."

"So then, what does Little Red Riding Hood write about?"

"I think she writes about wolves."

"Really?"

"Honestly. Little Red Riding Hood writes about how to tell the difference between grandmas and wolves. It's a kind of how-

to book."
  "Really?"
  "I think so."


On weekends, we go to a forest outside town.

There, raccoon dogs, weasels and smaller rodents, and even smaller insects, all live happily in that green cradle, grown thick with the leaves of chestnut oaks, white oaks, and snowbells. In the small swamps that dot the edges of the forest there are bitterlings, carp, and narrowhead grey mullet. They survey their watery realm with satisfaction and flutter their fins nonchalantly.

Through the forest wind many paths, which interweave like a maze. At the head of one path stands a lonesome sake brewery. This brewery, built of old materials and galvanized sheet metal, has started to become part of the forest. Ivy grows on the walls, and the roof is covered with leaves from big oak branches. From the factory emanates a low moan: *knock-knock-whoosh*.

I wore faded cotton shorts and a T-shirt that said KSC (short for Kennedy Space Center, a souvenir gift from someone), and I was running. I can't run the way I used to, but I can still run for about an hour if I keep to a slow pace of about six minutes per half mile. Yuji followed me on his bicycle. He only recently learned to ride without training wheels, and he's still a bit wobbly.

There were lots of fallen leaves on the path, roots poked up through the ground, and broken branches were scattered around. I have a light step and can spring over these obstacles, but Yuji has to dismount at each one and push the bike past them. He yelled at my receding figure: "Takkun, wait up! Don't leave me here!"

  "I wouldn't leave you here."
  "I know."
  "Come on, let's go."

We picked up the pace and headed for the middle of the forest.

We kept going for forty minutes, as if tracing each path with a single pencil line. Finally, we came to the ruins of a factory. Concrete jutted up from the earth. We could see the remains of plinths that once supported giant machines. On a wide limestone surface stood the solitary remnant of a building. It was mostly crumbled, but there was a door in it. And a tilted mailbox. Like this:

It was impossible to tell whether it had been the No. 5 factory, or the No. 5 warehouse, but the far side of the wall was completely gone.

Yuji always finds bolts and nuts and rivets and coil springs here. Sometimes he even finds small sprockets. Those are special days.

Mio used to come here too.

Yuji has enjoyed this activity ever since he was about two years old. Even so, there are still bolts and nuts and rivets and coil springs everywhere. It's strange, but these little parts are always here.

In an empty lot near our apartment, Yuji digs a hole and buries his newfound treasure. No doubt there must be quite a lot of parts there by now. If we piled them up on the ground, I bet they would be a foot deep.

Someday, somebody will dig them up. I sure would like to be there to see the look on their face.

"Can I ask you something?" I asked Yuji.

"What?"

"Why do you do this?"

He looked at me as if he were looking at somebody really, really stupid.

"You know why," he said. "Because it's fun."

Hmmph.

It was about one week before Mio left for Archive. It comforts me somehow to say it that way.

She said something like this: "Soon I won't be with you any longer, but when the rainy season returns, I will come back to see how the two of you are getting along."

A cold rain was falling on that June day.

"Until then," she said, "I'm asking you a big favor. By that time Yuji will be in elementary school, so be sure to see him off to school. Make sure he eats breakfast every day, and check the things he has with him to make sure he hasn't forgotten anything."

"Can you do it?"

"I can do it," I said.

"Really? When I come back, if you aren't doing things right I will never forgive you."

Then she gave a little smile. A smile so small I could easily have missed it.

"I worry about you," Mio said.

"We'll be fine," I said. "I'll be strong. I'll be a fine dad. Don't worry."

"Really?"

"Really."

"Promise."
"Uh-huh."

Have I gotten strong?
Have I become a good dad?
Soon it will be the rainy season.
A June Monday.
Today, once again, we will fly into a new day.

# 3.

"Yuji, breakfast is ready."

"Huh?"

"Hurry up and eat."

"Wha'?"

Yuji is wearing just his underwear and still has his eyes closed as I pull a T-shirt over his head.

"Breakfast. Breakfast."

"Mmm."

"Did you check your backpack? Have you forgotten anything?"

"Mmm. Nothing."

But every day he forgets something.

"Takkun?"

"What?"

"Fried eggs and wieners again?"

"That's right. It's delicious and nutritious."

"But it's the same thing every day."

"What?"

"Nothing."

"Hurry. You only have eight minutes."

"Really?" he said. Then, "Hey, Takkun?"

"Huh?"

"This T-shirt has a ketchup stain on it."

"You don't have to worry about that. Just think of it as the shirt's design."

"Really?"

"I haven't done the laundry lately, so I don't have another one to give you. This other one has a brown sauce stain, and the last one has curry all over it."

"Wow."

"If you were a neater eater that might help."

"Well, okay. I'll be fine with this shirt."


Returning from my errands, I got caught in the rain. It was the first time it had rained this month. When I got back to the office, Ms. Nagase brought me a towel, and she dried my shoulders and back.

"This suit…" Ms. Nagase said.

"Huh?"

Ms. Nagase appeared to become terribly confused about what she had started to say. She tugged on the collar and sleeves of her own blouse, as a way of protecting herself.

"What is it?"

"Well…" she began. "It might stain."

"Hmm, I suppose it might."

This did not appear to reassure her.

I smiled as if to say, *What?* but she shook her head as if to say, *Nothing.*

I handed her some papers and said, "Goodbye."

She muttered, "Thanks for your hard work," and hugged the papers to her chest.

The boss was at his desk, sleeping peacefully.

In the evening, under an umbrella, Yuji and I went out shopping.

"What would you like to eat tonight?"

"Curry rice."

"I'm bored with curry rice."

"What do you mean, 'bored'?"

"I mean it lacks imagination."

"What does that mean?"

"It seems to be the only menu item for our family meals."

"Really?"

"Really."

"So, what do you wanna do?"

"How would you like to try eating something we have never made before?"

"Wow, sure."

"Let's turn over a new leaf."

"What do you mean by that?"

"It's something an American president said a long time ago. Now his son is president."

"Really?"

"Really."

This was the start of a lively exchange of views, culminating in the selection for this evening's menu something that had heretofore never graced our table: stuffed cabbage. We divided responsibilities in buying the ingredients at the shopping center, and we were getting into a great mood. "New leaf, new leaf," Yuji kept repeating.

In Park No. 17, Nombre was sitting, as always. He had his black umbrella up, and he was gazing at the hydrangeas that bloomed all around the pond. Pooh, who hated the rain, had crawled under the bench.

"Nombre-sensei."

When I called to him, he turned to me and smiled.

"Hydrangeas?"

"They are beautiful things, aren't they? They blossom beautifully for those who look at them. That is their straightforward, unwavering nature."

Nombre continued. "Hydrangeas originally grew near the sea. That may be why they seem to have an affinity for water."

Even now, he might be chasing after the image of the woman with whom he had never formed a real bond. That may be the same as loving. Even someone you may not have seen for decades, someone who may no longer be on this planet, can still be missed.

"How's your book coming along?" he asked.

"I haven't started yet. Whenever I try to start writing, it's just hard. Even though there're so many things I want to write about."

"You can just wait until that time comes."

"'That time'?"

"That's right. The time when all the words that fill your mind just come tumbling out."

"Is that so?"

"That's right. It should come. That time."

Yuji was crouched down, saying something to Pooh under the bench. Pooh was listening in silence. If you lowered your head and listened carefully, you could hear Yuji saying, "Say, have you heard about the new leaf?"

We went home, and with the help of Yuji and the recipe, I

made stuffed cabbage. At the top of the recipe, it said, "A fool-proof meal."

But we managed to mess it up.

"Say…" said Yuji.

"What?"

"Is this what stuffed cabbage is supposed to taste like?"

"Actually, I don't think so."

"Well…"

"Hmm?"

"This is really bad."

"I think so too."

Five seconds of silence.

"I…"

"Yeah?" I said.

"I noticed something."

"What?"

"I think we made a mistake when we were shopping."

"What was it?"

"Instead of cabbage, I may have picked up lettuce."

"Well then."

Another five seconds of silence.

"Sorry."

"It's okay. Don't worry about it. It's just as much my fault for not noticing when I was cooking."

"Really?"

"Really."

I remember reading an article in the newspaper that said one in three English children cannot tell the difference between cabbage and lettuce. My own little English prince seems to be one of those one in three.

Maybe I am too.

# 4.

I knew that *Momo* was playing at the movie theater in the next town. This was an independent movie theater that generally played classic old films. This month, though, it was featuring a series of films based on Michael Ende books.

This week was *Momo*, and next week would be *The NeverEnding Story*.

Yuji said he would like to see *The NeverEnding Story*.

"You know Dad never goes into movie theaters, right?"

"I know."

"So you know that if you want to see the film, you'll have to watch it by yourself. Will you be okay?"

"I'll be okay."

"Then we can go on Saturday."

"Awright, Takkun. Thanks."

"You're welcome."

On Saturday, we left the apartment an hour before the movie started. I got on the old bicycle I use for riding to work, and Yuji got on his kid's bike, and we took the road that goes through the rice fields. The next town is about six miles away, so I thought we had plenty of time.

I can't take buses or trains.

If I get on a bus or train, as soon as the door closes, in the instant it starts to accelerate, the switch flips inside me, the bulb goes on, and the gauge maxes out.

It doesn't matter what kind of vehicle it is, they're all the same, even the monkey train in the amusement park, or a swan boat at some tourist spot. It's always the same. Buses and trains are bad, and monorails and cable cars (because of the elevation) are even worse. This is speculation, but I think airplanes would be totally unbearable. Submarines would be a death sentence.

I find it horrible to even contemplate cramming myself into a chamber where I could hardly move, with explosives under my butt to blow me into space.

That's why Kudryavka, the Russian dog who went around the earth aboard Sputnik, is my hero. I wish I had even a speck of her courage.

At any rate, this is incredibly inconvenient. Of all the limitations I have to bear, this is one of the most extreme. Because of this I will never be able to go to the moon, and I will never be able to dive the Marianas Trench.

This is most unfortunate.


We got to the theater five minutes before the movie started. It took longer than I thought because we were riding into a headwind. Yuji lowered his head and pedaled as hard as he could, but still we arrived at our destination much later than planned.

I handed him the sandwiches we had brought from home and a cola I bought from a vending machine. Our plan had been to eat together before the movie started, but there was no time.

At the entrance, I bought one child's ticket.

"Okay then. Have a good time."

Yuji seemed a bit uneasy because of the sudden change in plans. I took a few coins from my wallet and put them in his pants pocket.

"If the sandwiches aren't enough to fill you up, you can buy some popcorn. Or a donut would be okay, whatever you'd like to eat."

"Okay."

Yuji just stood there, clutching the lunchbox with the sandwiches and the can of cola, and didn't move.

The buzzer sounded announcing that the movie was about to begin. Yuji turned his head and looked at the door that led into the theater. Then he turned again and looked at my face.

"Go ahead. It's going to start."

I reached out and touched his shoulder to encourage him. I handed the ticket to the attendant and nudged Yuji in the back. He looked back at me twice and disappeared into the theater.

I wished I could have gone with him.

But I cannot enter a movie theater.

I can't go to musical concerts either, or to anybody's wedding. The reason for this is a little different from the reason I can't get into an elevator or go up in a tall building.

Naturally, I find all of this quite unreasonable. But what can I do? I'm stuck in the grip of a certain maddening impulse.

Whenever I find myself in a place where there are a lot of people who must all remain silent, I have an annoying urge to start talking loudly. I think everybody probably has this feeling to some extent, but it's all a matter of degree.

Things like, "Wow, that's a great painting!" or "Shit, just a little more woulda done it." Nothing really meaningful. Just the words that pop into my head, looking for an exit, causing problems for me. After that it's always the same pattern. My own confusion flips the switch, the bulb goes on, and the gauge maxes out.

It doesn't happen so much now, but when I was in college it was really a problem.

During class, I would actually break out in a greasy sweat, just trying to keep the words inside that would pop into my head: "Wow, that's really awful!" or "I don't remember anybody ever saying that."

That was the biggest reason I never finished college.

After I watched Yuji disappear, I walked around looking for a place to pass the time. The area was full of boutiques and accessory shops and fast food places all butting up against one another. I was worried that all this jostling could make me dizzy, but I had to wait until Yuji's movie was over. I had given him all the sandwiches, and I was hungry.

I walked around for a while, until I thought, *Here would be fine,* and decided to go to Starbucks. Lucky for me, all Starbucks are non-smoking. Because I'm so sensitive, tobacco smoke is a threat comparable to pepper gas.

If a bunch of people like me were to hold a demonstration (with placards saying, "Wow, that painting is great!" or "Shit, just a little more woulda done it!"), all the police would need to do is show up smoking cigarettes. The tears would stream from our eyes and we would run away, yelling "Wow, that's really awful!"

I can't drink coffee (the switch goes *Click!*), so there are only a few things at Starbucks I can put in my mouth. So I ordered a bottle of mineral water and a BLT.

I picked up the tray with my sandwich and drink and sat at a table in the back of the cafe. The place was about eighty percent filled with customers. There were a lot of people drinking coffee while doing something else: women in pantsuits sat facing laptop computers, boys who looked like students had textbooks open in front of them. Mimicking them, I opened the college notebook I had brought with me. I pressed the end of a mechanical pencil against my chest to expose some lead, took a big bite of my sandwich, and thought for a bit.

I took a big gulp and opened the notebook to the first page and wrote the number one. I meant to think of a title later, so I didn't write one.

The first words came out quickly.

*When Mio died, this was how I thought.*

After that, it was like writing down sentences I had already thought up, and the words just tumbled out of me.

How about that, I thought. This is just the way Nombre said it would be.

"When all the words that fill your mind just come tumbling out."

I wrote about Archive, and about Yuji, and about my work at the office, and about Nombre and Pooh, and about running on the weekend and the factory ruins. I thought I should start out by writing about our life now, and then gradually switch to writing about my memories of Mio.

Until now I had never written anything more than a diary entry, but I found that the sentences flowed. In my head I kept thinking about the books of John Irving, an author I really like, and about Kurt Vonnegut, the science fiction writer who taught him how to write sentences, and these were my references as I wrote.

Yuji and I, as described in the notebook, seemed to be much happier than the real Yuji and me.

I didn't have to write about the really hard things. That way, they could be happy. It was more fun to write about happy stuff.

I fell into a reverie, giving space and time and words to the "us" in the book. The time I gave them was, in other words, also time I myself lost.

The unbelievable thing was, by the time I looked up, the sun was low in the sky.

I was surprised.

"Aargh!"

With a jolt, I knocked over my bottle of water (thankfully, it was mostly empty). The other customers in the shop eyed me quizzically.

I hurriedly packed the college notebook and the mechanical pencil and the eraser in my bag, cleared my tray, and dashed out of the cafe. As I ran I glanced at my watch and realized the movie had ended over an hour before.

"Forgetting things that should not be forgotten."

I know this about myself, but some things must absolutely not be forgotten.

Why am I like this?

How did I get like this?

Several times I bumped into people around me, each time saying, "Excuse me," in my hurry to get back to Yuji.

Around the movie theater there was no sign of anybody. It was the middle of the next showing, a time when a strange quiet envelops movie theaters.

It wasn't long before I found Yuji.

He was sitting by himself in the middle of the wide main staircase.

On his lap he had the lunchbox, and he was hugging it, and staring dreamily at some undefined spot on the ground. His little mouth was moving as if he were singing, but I couldn't hear his voice.

"Yuji."

He did not respond to the sound of my voice. He didn't see me until I got up close to him.

His eyes were red, his nose was red, and his cheeks were red. He sniffled several times.

"I'm so sorry," I said.

"Mmm," said Yuji.

I plopped down, and with my finger I wiped the teardrops from Yuji's eyelashes. I took a tissue from my pocket and let him blow his nose.

"Remember, one side at a time. If you blow too hard you'll hurt your ears."

"Mmm."

I sat beside him.

"I'm really sorry."

"Mmm."

I held Yuji's little hand. As always, his hand was warm and a bit damp.

"I was worried," Yuji finally said in a nasal voice. "That something had gone wrong with you somewhere, and you couldn't move."

"Really?"

"Yeah. So I ran around looking for you. In lots of places. But I couldn't find you."

"I'm sorry," I said again.

"But it's okay," Yuji said. "You were okay, weren't you?"

"I was okay. But I did something awful to you."

Yuji shook his head. "I'm fine. I can take it."

"Yeah. You're terrific."

"Me? Terrific?"

"Yeah, really. You're way more terrific than I am."

"That's not true," Yuji said. "I cried. I cried a lot." And at that, he started crying again. I tousled his sweaty amber hair and pulled him close to me.

"I'm sorry for making you cry."

He held in his sobs and cried quietly, and with his head pressed to my chest he whispered to me under his breath, "Please. Don't leave me alone. Don't forget me."

I had probably given Yuji a bad experience he would never forget, and this was payback. As a result of this, I was to cause him further bad moments in the future.

About halfway home, I started to go a little crazy.

Yuji was himself again, and haltingly he was telling me the story of the film he had seen. The wind was at our backs, and we were making good progress, like boats under sail.

By the time I realized it, the situation had gotten pretty bad. Deep in my sinuses there was a smell as if something was burning, and my toes and fingertips were numb. On top of that, I felt terribly cold.

Despite all that, for a while I was following Yuji's story and dropping in an encouraging word here and there. But the gist of what he was saying wasn't really penetrating.

I managed to go on like this for about five minutes, but then I reached my limit.

"Yuji," I said, interrupting him.

"What is it?"

"Stop your bike."

"Okay."

We stopped our bikes on a path that extended at a right

angle from the asphalt road. I collapsed on the spot to a seated position.

Zero energy. Out of gas.

For most people this would just mean an empty stomach, but it's in my nature that everything is a big deal. So these symptoms were a big deal too. My arms and legs were now entirely numb. I could no longer sit upright, so I lay down on the ground. To prevent things like this from happening, I ordinarily eat five small meals a day. Today, however, I had been distracted, and I had completely forgotten my three o'clock meal.

"Takkun, are you okay?"

"Hmmm, I seem to be having a little problem."

"Really?"

"Yuji."

He squatted down, bringing his face close to mine.

"What?"

"Do you still have some money in your pocket?"

"Sure. I bought a bag of popcorn, but I still have money left."

"Well then, I have a favor to ask you."

"Sure."

"I want you to get back on your bike, by yourself, and go to the convenience store over there and buy something to eat and bring it to me."

"Something to eat?"

"That's right. My batteries have run out. I need new batteries to get moving again."

"Really?"

"Yeah. Can you do it?"

"Sure I can."

"Well then. Off you go."

"Got it."

Yuji got up and pushed his kid's bike to the asphalt. He

hopped on the saddle and looked back at me.

"Takkun?"

"Yeah."

Yuji's nose was red again. "Takkun, you won't die?"

"I'm fine, I won't die or anything."

"Really?"

"Really."

Yuji seemed to be weighing the truth of my words, and for a while he just looked at my eyes. It cost me great effort, but I managed a smile.

"Okay. I'll be right back," Yuji finally said.

"Okay. I'm counting on you."

Yuji stepped on the pedals and took off.

"Yuji!"

Yuji stopped the bike, brakes screeching.

"What is it?"

"I think you know this, but it isn't batteries I want you to buy."

"Huh?"

His "huh?" is a kind of conditioned response, and extracting the exact meaning can be tricky. But what else was I supposed to do?

"I want you to buy me something to eat. Something sweet would be good."

"Okay."

"If you can."

"Huh?"

"An ice-cream sandwich would be fine."

"Got it. That's something you like, isn't it, Takkun."

"Ah."

"I'll be right back."

"Okay."

He gave the pedals a full turn and distanced himself from me at surprising speed. I got a little flustered and tried to call out to him again, but I remembered his poor hearing and thought better of it.

"Don't go so fast..."

I lay down on the ground again.

"It's dangerous..."

The only things tethering me to the real world were the smell of the grass and the cold of the ground I could feel on my back. Falling into semi-consciousness, I continued to pray for Yuji's safety.

Over and over, a vision of him hit by a car flashed through my mind, each time causing spasms of pain.

My heart was beating out a tremolo rhythm—with occasional irregularities. It was really painful.

In my heart I called out, "Mio."

There was no answer.

"Mio."

Just for the heck of it I called out once more, but still there was no answer. Without knowing why, I was very sad.

"Takkun?"

I came to at the sound of Yuji's voice.

"I bought you an ice-cream sandwich."

He was dripping with sweat, and his shoulders shook with his breathing.

"I'm relieved," I said.

"About what?"

"Mmm, it's okay. But from now on you shouldn't go so fast on your bicycle."

"But..."

"No buts. It's okay. Thanks."

I raised half my body, and ate the ice-cream sandwich he had bought for me. It was very cold and made me shiver. I wished I had asked for something warm, but I ate it without complaint.

It would take time for the ice cream to be broken up and absorbed and carried throughout my body. I lay back down, facing the sky. Yuji lay down next to me.

The sky was already covered with a curtain of deep indigo. The stars were dancing like little lanterns whose batteries were flickering out.

"Are you okay?" Yuji asked.

"Yeah, I'll be all right in a minute."

"Oh?"

"Yeah."

"Well then…"

"What is it?"

"We should sing a song."

"What do you mean?"

"One that Mom taught me."

"I don't know it."

"That's okay."

"What do you mean it's okay? What is it?"

"Anything's okay, right?"

"Sure."

"When you're afraid, or when you get hurt, you can sing this and it'll make you feel better."

"Mom taught you this?"

"That's what I said."

"Well then, teach it to me."

Then, in a clear, thin voice, he began to sing.

*One elephant began to play*
*Upon a spider's web one day,*
*He found it such tremendous fun*
*That he called for another elephant to come.*

*Two elephants began to play*
*Upon a spider's web one day,*
*They found it such tremendous fun*
*That they called for another elephant to come.*

"Hang on a minute."

"What?"

"How many elephants end up in this song?"

"As many as you want. Until you feel better."

In my mind I pictured hundreds of elephants, all playing in a gigantic spider's web.

"Do you think the elephants were really having a good time?"

"Don't you? Isn't that why they call their friends?"

Hmmph.

"Sing with me. That'll make you feel better."

"I got it."

*Three elephants began to play*
*Upon a spider's web one day,*
*They found it such tremendous fun*
*That they called for another elephant to come.*

We continued singing until there were sixty-five elephants caught in the spider's web. And finally this is what we sang.

*Sixty-five elephants began to play*
*Upon a spider's web one day,*
*But sad to say the web gave way*
*And that was the end of a perfect day.*

"Takkun, are you feeling better?"

"Huh?"

"What?"

"It worked. When I stopped thinking about it, I got better."

"Really?"

"Yeah."

"It's cool, isn't it?"

"It sure is."

"We're late too, so let's go home, shall we?"

"Yeah."

Side by side, we walked the night road, pushing our bicycles along. The frogs were croaking loudly. I wonder if something good had happened to them.

"I'd like to see Mom again," Yuji said.

"I know what you mean."

After a while, Yuji spoke again. "Was it my fault Mom died?"

"No. Not at all."

"Really?"

"Really. What made you think that?"

"Nothing in particular."

After another while, I said, "It really wasn't."

"I know."

"Okay then."

"Yeah."

I know someday the time will come when he will learn what really happened. In any group of people there will always be those who like to gossip. Right now he's rather foggy about all this, but he has begun to grasp a little bit of the truth. Probably some busybody told him something. He's too young to really understand though. I think that for a while I will continue to lie to him. If at all possible, I think it would be best if he first learned the truth when he reads this book.

The fact is, saying "It's Yuji's fault that Mio died" is not quite the truth. Given a certain result in the present, it is difficult to say what the actual specific cause may have been.

What is certain is that the roulette ball fell in the Black 13 space. But why? A simple explanation for this is not possible. I'm doing my best to make sure this roulette wheel does not change our world.

What is certain is that Yuji's was a difficult birth.

Mio had suffered a number of problems during her pregnancy, which left her weak by the time of the birth, and she had been shot up with all kinds of needles. We had considered a C-section, allowing Yuji to emerge through a chasm opened by the doctor's hand instead of the birth canal, but in the end, after a thirty-hour labor, he arrived into this world by the conventional route. He was a healthy baby and weighed almost eight pounds.

His mother's strength, on the other hand, was severely depleted. All the organs of her body, the organs that filter, break down, and neutralize things, no longer functioned well.

She left this planet five years after that, and even now I don't fully understand the relationship between the difficulties she endured at that later time and the multiple functional breakdowns she suffered at the time of Yuji's birth. After the birth she became really healthy again, and she lived a normal life as a normal wife and mother. So I cannot truthfully say it was Yuji's fault that Mio died.

Even if it is true that something connected to the birth took her life five years later, this does not mean that Yuji is to blame.

He didn't do anything.

It was the wishes of both Mio and me that brought him into this world. At that time, he had not yet drawn a breath, had not yet opened his eyes. He was as pure as snow that had not yet touched the ground.

For this reason, Yuji must never be allowed to suffer on this account.

# 5.

The following day, we went to the forest as usual.

Like always, the old sake brewery was making its knock-knock-whoosh noise. The sky was covered with thick gray clouds. The wind that came from deep in the woods smelled of rain.

"We might get wet."

"Huh?"

I slowed my pace and let Yuji catch up.

"It smells like rain. We might get wet."

Yuji sniffed a few times.

"I can't tell."

"Let's go a little faster." Our habit was to go out of our way, to add some distance before visiting the factory ruins, but today we took the shortest possible route to our destination.

It was dark in the woods. The oak and snowbell leaves covered our heads like a canopy. Layers of fallen leaves made a comforting sound as we trod on them.

No birds were singing. It may be that the sky was too gloomy for them to have anything to say.

It was quiet.

At times, the wind would stir as if it had just remembered to blow, shaking the treetops and making a sound like beans being thrown. A fallen tree that hadn't been there the last time lay blocking the path. I helped Yuji lift his bicycle over it.

At last the forest ended, and we arrived at the factory ruins. The sky grew even darker.

The first drop grazed my cheek and fell to my shoulder.

"Here it comes."

The rain soon grew stronger, wetting the concrete and giving off a smell redolent with memories. In all the ruins of this once huge factory, there was no nook where we might take shelter. Staying out in the woods would be better.

I decided we should go back the way we came. "We should go back," I said to Yuji.

But he didn't hear me. He thrust out his forehead, drenched with rain. With a stern expression he was staring intently at something. Eyes squinting and eyebrows drawn together, for him a very grown-up expression, Yuji gazed ahead with his whole heart and soul.

I turned to see what he was staring at.

In the gray, rain-misty landscape, a single spot of pale color stood out. It was right in front of the last remaining bit of wall with the door labeled No. 5. I wiped the drops from my eyelashes with my fingertip and took another good hard look. In an instant I recognized a familiar silhouette.

There was no mistaking what I was seeing.

It was Mio.

With a cherry blossom pink cardigan draped over her shoulders, she crouched in front of the door. Slowly I looked down at Yuji. He looked up at me. He opened his eyes wide and opened his mouth in an "O."

As if wanting to hold an especially private conversation, in a tiny, tiny whisper he said to me, "What do we do now, Takkun?"

He kept blinking, many times, nervously.

"Mom…"

"Mom came back down from Archavie."

Trembling, we approached her. Not because we were afraid. This was no husband fearing his own wife's ghost. It was because it seemed even something like a tiny puff of air could erase her existence.

Yuji was probably thinking the same thing. He did not run straight to her side and hug her.

It could be that he was instinctively aware of the fleeting nature of happiness.

I, on the other hand, as an upstanding adult, was not forgetting the need to find a rational explanation.

The Doppelgänger Theory.

A completely unknown person who could be a twin. A real twin who would not be a completely unknown person. If this was some stranger, she looked so much like Mio it was as hard to believe as if she were a ghost; if this was a twin there was no reason I wouldn't know about her. Mio had a younger sister and brother, but they looked nothing like her. On the contrary I, who was no blood relation, looked much more like an older brother to Mio. I had never heard any talk of a twin sister locked away somewhere, behind a mask.

The theory that she had really been alive the whole time.

I don't think so.

This is a very seductive line of thinking, but I don't think it's possible.

If it were true, that would mean I had stood by the deathbed of some other woman, gone to the funeral of some other woman, talked to the grave of some other woman.

I am not that much of an idiot.

Other theories came to me—the Alien Theory, the Clone Theory—things that David Duchovny, I mean, Fox Mulder might believe, but I had a hard time believing them.

This is what I was thinking as I approached her, one step at a time, but what emerged as the most plausible theory was that this woman standing in front of me was in fact the ghost of my wife.

I mean, she had even told me, "When the rainy season returns, I will come back to see how the two of you are getting along."

She had kept her promise—on a rainy day in June, she had come back to us.

When I had gotten so close I could almost reach out and touch her, I saw clearly. The woman crouching had two tiny moles on her right earlobe. And the white tips of her eyeteeth peeked from between her closed lips.

This was not someone who looked a lot like Mio, this was not a twin sister, this was not a clone.

This was Mio herself.

If you think that expression is in error, I could put it another way. This was an entity equipped with the heart, appearance, and probably also the memories of Mio. If this was a ghost she was very real, with crisp contours, and on top of that she smelled really good.

That familiar scent of her hair.

I have nothing else to compare it to, so all I can say is "that scent." It was like some intimate message she transmitted to me alone.

It was the only message like it in the world.

I was receiving it again now.


She made no sign of having noticed us, but was looking absent-mindedly at the drops of rain at her feet. Looking more closely, I could see that her cheeks were a bit plumper than when she had left us. This was her face as it had been before she got so sick. She looked healthier, and younger.

I thought this was a little odd.

A healthy ghost is an oxymoron, like an altruistic financier, or a positive-thinking Woody Allen. Maybe when ghosts return to Earth, they are able to show the happiest form they ever had as people.

Beneath her cherry blossom pink cardigan she wore a plain white dress. Could this be the clothing supplied on the planet Archive? Could it be that the people there all wear white clothing? People have always thought that ghosts wear white, but wouldn't they have changed to something more contemporary by now?


Yuji was unable to stand it any longer, and called to her in a small, trembling voice.

"Mom?"

Mio looked up and saw us for the first time. She stared blankly with a neutral, dispassionate gaze. Slowly she closed her eyes, opened them again, and then tilted her head a little.

Each one of these gestures was so familiar, so precious for me,

I felt like I was going to cry. If this was a ghost it was identical to my wife. And of course I felt the same love for her.

Tentatively I extended my hand, as if to verify her existence. She seemed to become a bit frightened, and her body stiffened.

Was something wrong? Might it be against the rules to be touched by a human being?

But I was unable to restrain my action, and I touched her on the shoulder.

I thought something would happen, but nothing did.

In my hand I felt her thin shoulder, wet with rain. She was somehow glowing with a faint warmth. I remember feeling slightly surprised. I might have found it easier to accept had I found myself clutching something colder than the June rain, or a cherry blossom pink mist instead of the shoulder I actually felt in my hand.

No matter, here she was, exuding that wonderful scent, and my heart was pounding violently.

Yuji had also made his way slowly up to her, put out his small hand, and cautiously clutched the sleeve of her cardigan. She started to smile at him, but her cheek stiffened, leaving an expression that was only half a smile.

What was it—this feeling of strangeness?

I became a bit unsettled and tried saying her name.

"Mio?"

She looked at me, and her lips parted softly, exposing her large eyeteeth.

"Who is Mio?" she said. "Is that my name?"

It was the same familiar voice, thin and high, with a slight tremble at the end of a word.

The familiarity of her voice made me want to cry all the more, but the meaning of what she had said shocked me enough to pull the tears right back in.

"What do you mean, 'Is that my name?'" I said. "Don't you know your name?"

"Hmm?" said Yuji.

"It seems so," Mio said.

"Really?" said Yuji.

"I...I don't remember anything."

"What do you mean, 'anything'?" I was moving my hands around and around in the air, pointlessly. "Anything?"

"That's right." A self-mocking smile came across her face, as if she were disappointed at a fortune she had just picked from a box at a shrine.

"So?" she asked. "Who are you two?"

"What do you mean, 'who?'" I asked her, still with that unsettled feeling. "I am your husband, and Yuji is your son."

"That's right. Son," Yuji said.

"That can't be," she said.

"But it is," I said.

"It really is," said Yuji.

"Just a moment." As if to stop our words in their tracks, she held out the palm of one hand, and with the other she held her head. "You were already here when I noticed you."

She closed her eyes, and with a serious expression, reeled in her memory.

"It must have been about ten minutes ago. I had been thinking for a long time, but I can't remember a thing. Not where this is, not why I'm here, or even who I am, sitting here thinking."

Hearing this made me think. She had alighted on this spot just ten minutes ago. At that time, it seems, she had somehow left all her memories behind on Archive.

Which must also mean (perhaps?) that she doesn't even realize she's a ghost.

It's so confusing and I can't figure it out.

"So, today, did I come here with you two?"

"That's right," I said, making a snap judgment.

"Huh?" said Yuji.

I gripped his skinny neck. He shut up.

"We all came here together. It's our regular Sunday stroll."

"Really?"

"Yeah," I said, nodding. "And then Yuji and I were off in the woods for a few minutes, and when we came back you were like this. You must have fallen and smacked your head on something."

"You mean the shock of a fall gave me amnesia?"

"It seems so."

"Really?" asked Yuji.

I gripped his neck harder. He shut up.

"Anyway, let's go home. I'm sure your memory will come back soon."

"I wonder."

"I'm sure."

She stood up slowly. Her damp dress clung to her hips, and droplets fell from her sleeves.

"Let's hurry home. You'll catch cold."

"Okay."

She will be happier knowing nothing. There was no need to make her recall unhappy memories.

I was remembering something she had said. Her last words to me had been, "When the rainy season returns, I will come back." She had said that.

"That's right. Together with the rain I will visit, to make sure you both are doing all right, and then before summer comes I will go back again. You know I don't like the heat."

If she had forgotten where she had come from, maybe she would also forget about going back to Archive. Then we could stay together forever.

Me and Yuji and Mio. The three of us.

If we could all be together, the fact that Mio was a ghost would not be a major problem.

Really.

Yuji and Mio walked the wooded path side by side, and I brought up the rear, pushing the bicycle. At first Yuji was so excited it seemed he wouldn't be able to settle down, but at some point he found himself, and reached out his hand to Mio. As soon as she noticed she grasped his hand. Yuji relaxed and looked up into Mio's face. She smiled a gentle little smile. At that moment Yuji, who could no longer stand it, started crying out loud.

Understandable. He was touching his mother's hand for the first time in a year.

She turned back and looked at me as if to say, "What's all this about?"

"At some point I think you'll realize," I said. "Yuji's an awful big crybaby."

Having said this, I would be able to use it as an excuse in the future if Yuji started crying again for some strange reason.

"He's a little upset. About you losing your memory."

"Really?" Yuji asked, sobbing.

I ignored him and went on.

"Don't think about it too much, just be nice to him. As you always have been."

She nodded as if to say, "I get it," and then she reached out to touch Yuji's thin shoulder, and drew him to her and hugged him. He felt his mother's warmth, and he fell into a comfortable intoxication as if drunk on his own tears.

Yuji had already experienced a separation from his mother. This chance reunion with her might eventually lead to another day of parting, so sadness was foreordained.

"Before summer comes," she had said.

If those words were true, the time given us would be short.

I grabbed the sleeve of Mio's dress, pressed my face against her, and said softly to the sobbing Yuji, "Now is the time for us to be as nice to her as we possibly can."

# 6.

When we got back to the apartment, I took Mio to the back room and showed her what was in each of the drawers of the closet. Her clothing was all where it had been a year before.

Yuji and I changed our clothes in the front room, and then went into the bathroom. This was the only place I could think of where we could talk without Mio overhearing.

"Listen," I whispered. "Mom doesn't remember a thing."

"Really?"

"Really. She doesn't know about the time you and I have spent living on our own, and she doesn't remember anything about before she and I were married.

"And..." I started to say, but then I had to clear my throat quietly.

"And she doesn't remember that a year ago she got sick and had to leave this planet."

"Right."

"So, I think we should try to keep these things a secret."

"What things?"

"What do you mean, 'what things'? I want her to think that she has never gone away anywhere, that the three of us have been living together right here, in this apartment, the whole time."

"Yesterday too?"

"That's the idea."

"And the day before that?"

"That's right."

"So, if Mom asks me, what should I tell her?"

"Like what?"

"Anything."

"You'll do fine."

"I don't think I can do it."

"Then just cry and fool her. Just cry out loud and everything will be fine."

"Really?"

"Really. She went to all the trouble of coming back to us, so it would be better if she didn't know how sad it was when she left."

"I think so too."

"Right? If Mom were to know the truth, she might think she has to go back to Archive."

"I wouldn't want that."

"Right. So you know what you have to do."

"Got it. I'll try."

Like athletes pumped up for the game after a pep talk, we exchanged high-fives and I opened the bathroom door and went out.

Mio was standing right there.

I was very startled, but I pretended not to be. It was probably pretty apparent that I was only pretending.

Had she heard what we were saying? I looked at her face.

"Do the men of this house always go to the bathroom together?"

"Sometimes, sure. When we're in a hurry, sometimes we do. Like this time."

Dodged that bullet.

Judging by her face, she was a bit astonished.

"Well then, what is this?" She was pointing to the middle of the room.

"What do you mean, 'this'?"

"Why is all this stuff all over the place?"

"What do you mean, 'all over the place'?"

To me, everything looked fine, tidy, in its practical place. The clothes we planned to wear around the house that day were in a single pile in the north corner of the room. The laundry I had collected was in a heap next to that. Dirty clothes had been collected on the south side of the room so as not to get mixed up with the clean laundry. Books and comics that didn't fit on the shelves were lined up in plastic shopping bags, organized by author.

Next to the window were two bags of burnable trash that didn't get put out on the right day. But even with all that, I wouldn't say there was "stuff all over the place."

Everything was in its proper place, in accordance with a strict system.

"It's true there are a lot of things on the floor," I said. "But the way things are, every place has a meaning."

"Did I leave them this way?"

"Ah..." I said, and then, "No."

And that's the way it was. Once you start telling lies you're not used to, the cracks in the story are soon exposed.

"These…uh…I put them there."

I gained some time with little *ums* and head-scratching and *uhs* and throat-clearing.

"I'll tell you the truth. You haven't been well for quite a while, and you haven't been able to do any housework."

"Really?"

"Yeah. You haven't been able to get up for a week."

"So, I haven't been able to do any laundry, and that's why you're wearing those dirty clothes?"

I looked at the sweatshirt I had on.

"Is this dirty?"

"I wouldn't call it clean. How many days have you been wearing it?"

"This is only the third day."

"Well, if you ate a little more carefully it might not look so bad."

And then she pointed at the mountain of laundry.

"You have to beat these shirts a little bit before you dry them, or they end up all wrinkly."

"Beat them? How?"

Mio shook her head, as if to say "Enough."

"So, if I've been sick for a week, how come you took me for a walk to that place today?"

"Uh…rehab."

"Really."

"Yeah…sure."

"Sure?"

"It's something we do every week, and you said you were going to go even if you had to push yourself."

"I said that?"

"Yes, you did."

She let out a big sigh.

"I…" She put her hand to her chest and leaned her head close to me. "Am I really your wife?"

"Yes, you really are. Not 'maybe,' not 'I think so,' really really."

She made a face that seemed to suggest grave doubts about herself—and about why she would marry a man like me.

"Well, that went well." Better I had said nothing. She seemed to grow more uncertain, although whether about me or about herself I couldn't be sure.

"And what is our last name?"

"Aio."

"So, my name is Mio Aio?"

"That's right."

"Mio Aio."

"That's right."

"How old am I?"

"Twenty-nine. Same as me."

"Twenty-nine years old."

But the curtain had already come down on her life once, at twenty-eight. Twenty-nine was a future she was never supposed to have. And on top of that, the woman now in front of me seemed much younger.

Really young.

Kurt Vonnegut once wrote that people who have left us can choose whatever age they want to be.

In Vonnegut's novel *Jailbird,* his father appears as a nine-year-old kid in heaven. Vonnegut's father is relentlessly tormented by bullies, who pull down his pants. The bullies take his underwear and throw it down the mouth of hell, which looks like a well. Then from far below, you can hear the screams of Hitler and Nero and Salome and people like that.

This is what Vonnegut wrote:

"I could imagine Hitler, already experiencing maximum

agony, periodically finding his head draped with my father's underpants."

What I'm trying to say is, I'm glad my wife did not come back to me as a nine-year-old.

"How old is Yuji-kun?" she asked.

"Huh?" said a voice from the bathroom.

"Six. He's in the first grade," I answered.

It was strange to hear her refer to Yuji as "kun." It was as if she were someone very close, but not my wife. Like a cousin I had known since childhood.

"You're saying I'm a twenty-nine-year-old housewife with a six-year-old son."

"That's right."

"Somehow I don't feel that way at all."

"I see."

"And this means I was in love with you? Enough to marry you."

Her face said that this was the biggest puzzle of all.

"You may find it hard to believe, but it's true."

Somehow I too was beginning to lose confidence. Why would someone like her have chosen someone like me? Indeed, we were a strange match.

"How did we get to know each other?"

"In high school. When we were both fifteen. In the spring."

"We were in the same grade?"

"That's right. We were in the same class for three years."

A friendly smile came to her face.

"Do me a favor. Tell me about what we were like then."

"Sure."

I smiled my best smile, as if I were in the middle of an important meeting, and started to tell the tale of so long ago, of how we had met, and were happy, in the innocent Age of Mythology.

"When we met…" I began.

And then we heard the flush of a toilet, and Yuji emerged from the bathroom.

"Ahh, that feels better."

He had apparently just discharged a fundamental bodily function.

"And my boy's shirt?" Mio asked, as Yuji wiped his wet hands across his chest. "How many days?"

"The fourth, I think," I said, knowing it was the fifth.

"Really?"

"Really…I think."

"Couldn't you try to eat a little more carefully?"

"Yeah, it's a bit of a problem for him."

"For you too apparently."

"Oh."

So that night the two of us ate our dinner carefully.

On the menu was spaghetti with meat sauce that I threw together quickly. We did not let a single crumb of ground beef drop to the table, and of course our shirts stayed clean too.

Fantastic.

Mio ate her spaghetti as if it were nothing unusual. After that she went to the bathroom. I did not believe this was standard protocol for a ghost, but she showed no self-consciousness about it, and it might have been normal for all I knew.

After our meal, Mio said she was tired. She went into the back room, spread the futon, and lay down. She had been confused, and confusion can make people very tired.

Yuji hurriedly spread his futon next to hers and, hugging *Momo*, burrowed in. Just being beside her made him happy.

Seen from this room, he seemed to be pretending to read his book, all the while checking repeatedly on Mio beside him.

Once he had ascertained she was still there, he let a sigh of relief and happiness escape his little lips.

I took off my sweatshirt and threw it and Yuji's shirt into the washing machine.

It was not something I was particularly worried about, but apparently wearing clothing with cola or sauce stains was not conventional. Nobody had ever told me that. As long as Mio was here, clean, neatly folded clothes always just appeared before my eyes, without any effort on my part.

When it was just me and Yuji, I thought I was doing as much as I could, but as much as I thought I could do seemed to be less than fifty percent of what the world expected.

Somewhere in this wide world, there must be a completely flawless family without a mom, where the dad and the kid wear perfectly clean clothes without wrinkles or stains, and they live in places that look like clean rooms in silicon chip factories, without out a speck of dust, and on weekends the dad and the kid go in the car to a multiplex in the suburbs, and they stuff their faces with popcorn and watch Disney cartoons.

I had long ago given up wishing for things I shouldn't wish for or things I could never do. I am what is left after a lot of things are subtracted from a normal human being. And so I think I will never be able to bring up Yuji like a normal kid in a normal family.

But I try.

Sometimes I don't notice things I should notice, forget things I'm supposed to remember, and get tired and fall asleep without doing the things I'm supposed to do. Even so, I try to do a little better every day.

So how does she look at someone like me?

I can understand why she would want to come back to this planet to check on how Yuji and I are doing. If she could remember that, what would she say?

I bet she would sigh, and say, "Just as I thought."

But I'm sure she wouldn't say, "Wow, you really tried your best, didn't you?"

A little after ten o'clock, I took a shower and put on my pajamas. I always wake up several times during the night, so if I don't go to bed about this time, I'm really worthless the next day.

For me, sleep is like being a security guard patrolling a gigantic office building.

In the building there are thousands of rooms. When I find one with a little light peeking out from under the door, I grab the doorknob and go in. There's an antique TV set in the corner, and I sit down on the sofa. I pass the time by flipping through the channels and watching dreams that look a little bit like old B-movies. But some nasty person inevitably comes along and turns off the TV.

*Click.*

And so the night goes by.

*Click.*

I awaken to this sound and go off in search of the next dream.

*Click.*

*Click.*

It makes me very tired.

"How are you feeling?" I asked Mio in the next room.

She had a vacant look, and slowly she looked up, but not as far as my face. Her line of sight remained in a middle ground somewhere between Yuji and me.

"My head hurts."

"Are you feverish? You might have caught cold, getting so wet in the rain."

She nodded in a vague way, neither confirming nor denying.

"I wonder…"

"May I come over there to you?"

Going to her side in my pajamas like this seemed somehow a little indecent. I thought that of course because to her, emotionally, I was someone she had just met. And after a year, I was a bit shy myself.

"Don't be silly. It's your bedroom, isn't it?"

I walked over to where her pillow lay on the floor, knelt down, and laid my hand on her forehead. Can ghosts catch cold?

"You may have a fever. Just a slight one though."

"I'm okay. If I sleep it'll go away."

"Really?"

"Yeah." I felt very strange.

The sensation of her forehead. Warmth. Her scent.

We may have exchanged these same words in the past, this casual conversational refrain.

It seemed unreal that she had died a whole year before. Maybe I had been watching a dream like some Hollywood movie about somebody with a grave illness, and I had just woken up.

*Click.*

But her words said otherwise.

"He's a cute kid, Yuji-kun."

Hearing that made me sad, and in a dry voice I said to her, "He's your kid too, you know."

"That's right, I suppose. I just wish I could hurry up and remember that."

"Don't worry. It's okay."

"Yeah."

What if, I think. What if when she left this planet she left her memory behind. Her memory might still be somewhere in this room. If that were the case, it must have made problems for her on Archive. The inhabitants of that planet have to write books for the "Somebody."

People with no memories can't do anything but write about

the emptiness of not having a memory. That does not make a very interesting book.

We have to give her lots of memories to take back to Archive with her when it comes time for her to go back to that planet again. Then she'll be able to write about Yuji and me.

And "Somebody" will be able to read it.

Yuji had fallen asleep clutching *Momo* in his arms. His little mouth was open slightly, his thin eyelids with their blue veins were lowered, and he was sleeping happily. His nose was a little stuffed, and I could hear the thick sound of his sleeping breath.

The Happy Prince.

He must be having happy dreams.

Gently I tugged *Momo* from his arms and put it back in the colored box that served as his bookcase.

"Good night, then," I said to Mio beside him.

"Good night? Are you going somewhere else to sleep?"

"I'll spread my futon in the next room and sleep there."

Slowly she shook her head. "Sleep here. Beside Yuji. Isn't that where sleep every night? The three of us, all side by side?"

"Well, yeah, sure…"

Actually, that wasn't true. For a long time, it had just been the two of us.

Me and Yuji, side by side.

Like two spoons in a drawer.

"You don't mind? I mean, to you I must seem like some man you just met today."

"It's okay. I think my memory will come back to me more quickly if we just do what we've always done, what comes naturally."

It's possible you lost forever those memories you should remember always.

When you lost your life.

Those were the words on the tip of my tongue, but I swallowed them.

"Okay then. I will."

With Yuji between us, I spread my futon parallel to Mio's and lay down. I pulled the string to turn out the light, leaving on just the orange nightlight. Yuji often wakes up in the night to use the toilet, so I never darken the room completely.

For some reason, I was tense.

She didn't seem like a ghost at all, and my love for her was still singing loudly in my chest. A valiant aria: *Ho ho ho! Yo ho ho! Ho ho ho! Yo ho ho!*

"Takkun…" she said.

"Yeah?"

"About what we were talking about before…" she whispered, as if to say, "Tell me."

That voice was reeling in something inside me. And that something was spreading throughout my chest, welling up to the base of my throat, lapping at my sinuses, rising to the back of my eyelids, making me want to cry.

"Sure," I said. "I'll tell you more."


When we met, we were both fifteen, and the whole world was just yesterday, today, and tomorrow.

You understand, don't you? At that age, we did not look back at the past, and we had no interest in the future beyond tomorrow.

You were a terribly skinny girl.

Not that you were some genderless girl who looked more like a boy. You were like the spirit of a coffee spoon shaped like a girl. Your hair was very short, probably the shortest of anybody in the class—even the boys.

And you wore eyeglasses with silver wire frames.

For a girl of that age, that was the same as saying, "I have absolutely no interest in boys. So leave me alone."

I think I remember there were about three girls like that in our grade. Most people wouldn't wear eyeglasses to school, no matter how bad their eyesight was. Either they used contact lenses, or if they could put up with seeing poorly they just got by with their naked eyes.

That was fifteen years ago. We didn't have trendy eyeglasses like we have today, and fashionable girls simply didn't wear eyeglasses.

In some ways, then, you were obviously different from other people, especially other girls. Your head was two sizes smaller than your classmates', and your small face made your eyeteeth look disproportionately large. At fifteen you certainly made an impression on me.

I was a simple sort, kind of gullible, taking whatever was right in front of my eyes at face value, including the signals you were emitting.

"I understand. I will never lay a hand on you."

Not that I ever laid a hand on any girl.

I have to say, though, that I was well aware of your charms.

More than anything, you were serious. Most people do not find seriousness attractive, but I liked serious people. I thought it was one of the greatest virtues, something that people should value more highly. Seriousness is related to trust, and trust is one of the most important elements that make up love. That's why serious people actually know more about love than carefree people do. I should know, because I am a serious person myself.

And, although I didn't realize it at the time, you had plenty of sensitivity, wisdom, and humor. Behind those glasses, reaching out a hand to me, was a sensitive girl waiting for true love.

On top of that, from a purely aesthetic standpoint, you were actually quite beautiful. The shape of your head, the curve from your neck to your jaw, were really quite something. Phrenologically, you were perfect. That might be the reason why so many people who drew pictures, or sculpted clay, asked you to model for them. You were often chosen to be in photographs, and you were also often the model for drawings I used to scribble in my textbooks.

At any rate, that was the you I met in the spring when I was fifteen.

We were in the same class, in the same group. I sat right behind you.

Classes got reshuffled every year, but you and I stayed in the same class, same group, and I sat either to the right of you, or to the left of you, or right behind you. You and I spent most of the hours of every day inside the same small circle less than six feet in diameter.

At that age we were just becoming aware of ourselves, that we were sexually maturing individuals, sowing the surrounding area with messages, locked in chemicals, that we were prowling for partners with whom we might create a legacy of children and grandchildren. The people receiving these messages, whether they were aware of it themselves or not, responded by emitting chemicals of their own. These were the messages of love exchanged below the level of consciousness.

The two of us, enclosed in our tight six-foot circle, traded these chemicals more often than anyone. Writing down in pencil the words on the blackboard, battling drowsiness as we listened to the teacher drone on, we exchanged many messages using this modest means of communication.

*"Is anybody there? Looking for a partner in love."*

We were completely ignorant of this intimate activity taking place. We never noticed it at all.

You, with your wire-frame glasses, were indifferent, the spirit of a coffee spoon that had nothing to do with love. Your short hair, your knee-length uniform skirt, your pierced ears and neck-laces and even your lip gloss, all seemed unconnected. In class you were an avid note-taker. Your eyes rarely wandered from a circuit of four points: the blackboard, the teacher, the textbook, and your notebook.

You were a model student in every sense of the word.

Fantastic.

The fact that you were not ordinarily one of the top students in the class, grade-wise, was an amusing commentary. You were not a genius, or even especially bright, you were simply serious and diligent. You were a straightforward person who often failed to grasp the key point. The people around you to whom you happily lent your notes often got better grades than you did. Your notes were clearly written, easy to read, and well organized. They were a big help to me too.

I often avoided the classroom or showed up without my books, and still managed to get decent grades thanks to your magic notes. Anybody who even skimmed your notes never found it hard to get a passing grade on a test. People with a little smarts could read them and figure out what the teacher was thinking. You, though, were not that smart, and you never managed to squeeze the same value out of your own notes as other people did. You always chose the route of steady progress, even if it took a little longer.

At some point, Mio had fallen asleep.

I closed my mouth and gazed at her sleeping face, bathed in the orange light. It was moving gently, in time with her breathing.

She was breathing. Just like she was really alive.

All of a sudden I recalled her final days, and pain coursed through my chest.

Would I lose her again?

I want to be by her side. Forever. Until the day I die.

I don't care if she is a ghost. I don't care if she has forgotten all about us.

As long as she wants to be with me, that's all I need.

Softly I said to her, "Good night."

Yuji answered, "Really?"

Of course, he was talking in his sleep.

**7.**

When I opened my eyes again she was already up and making breakfast.

"How are you? How are you feeling?"

"My head still hurts a little, but it's better than it was yesterday."

"You should just take it easy. I can fix breakfast."

"It's okay. Moving around like this helps me forget about it."

I washed my face, brushed my teeth, and sat down at the table.

"How about your memory?"

"Nothing new to report. Same as yesterday."

She put a plate of meatballs and scrambled eggs on the table.

"Sorry, but the breakfast menu is the same as lunch today."

"I don't mind. That's just normal for us. You realized right away though that I like to take a bento to work."

"The lunch box was in the dish rack."

"Oh, I see."

"Are you ready to eat?"

"When Yuji gets up, I'll eat with him. That's what we always do."

This was all a little too eerie, the illusion that I had spent the start of every day with Mio, yesterday and the day before, just like today.

She dried her hands on a hand towel and sat down across from me. She was wearing a yellow-green sweatshirt with the logo of the fitness club where she used to work. That was what she usually wore around the house. She had her long hair in a ponytail, as always. She has lots of hair, and the ponytail was bundled high near the crown of her head. That too was the way she had always worn it.

"Your hair…" I began. "Just like always."

At my words her face took on a pensive expression.

"So, you mean to say it's been some time since I put my hair in a ponytail?"

"Uh…" I said. "No."

"I just put it up because it was getting in my way when I was cooking."

"That's right. That must be it. That's it."

It's not that I was bad at lying, it was just a matter of memory. I had completely forgotten I was lying to her.

Seeing me flustered, she got a doubtful look on her face.

"Something seems strange."

"What do you mean?"

"I mean you."

"Ah," I said. "Me."

"Don't worry," I said. "There's nothing strange about me."

She let out a sigh, as if to say, "Well, all right."

"I cook here every day, don't I? For you and Yuji?"

She was looking at the gas burner, covered in greasy grunge, and the sink, stained and rusty.

"I guess so."

On the wall next to the stove were the scorched remains of my first and last attempt at making French fries. I left oil on the burner and forgot about it completely. The oil ended up sustaining some unbelievably big flames. I went a little nuts, filled a bucket with the previous night's bathwater from the tub, and threw it on the flames. Needless to say, that was a mistake. There was a big explosion, but miraculously the flames went out.

French fries were everywhere, turned to cinders. With all the excitement, I had a seizure and nearly fainted.

That was about three months ago.

"Takkun," she said.

"Yeah?"

"Last night, before I fell asleep, you were telling me you thought of me as 'serious.' You used that word over and over."

"Yes, I did. You were a serious girl."

"Looking at all this though, I think I must be a very lazy, sloppy person. The kitchen, the bathroom, the toilet—there's no sign they've been properly cleaned in a long time. The refrigerator has nothing but instant foods."

She looked at me with a smile that suggested she was on the verge of crying. "Model students don't always turn out to be model housewives."

"No, that's not it," I said. The words came out of me in a single burst.

She looked me in the eye, expecting more.

I said it again. "Really. That's not it."

Her pupils glazed over.

I had never found it easy to find the right words to convince anybody of anything. At times like this, I was apt to say the stupidest thing possible.

"Really."

I said it again, but in a small voice as if talking to myself. I tried to make up some likely reason, but it was amazing how much nothing I was able to think of.

"Someday I'll tell you," I said. "About this." I raised both arms to indicate the entire apartment. "There is a reason."

"Really?"

"Yeah."

When she had been with us, the apartment was not like this. The kitchen, the bathroom, the toilet were all sparkling clean, a pleasure to use, well taken care of. The refrigerator was always full of fresh foods, and there was not a single package of instant food to be found anywhere. It was I who had brought us to this. Without her notes I had never been capable of anything, and as an adult I was the same way. Without her, nothing went right.

"Your hair," she said, with that vague gaze of hers. "Shall I cut it tonight?"

"My hair?" I asked, twirling my curls in my fingers.

"When was the last time you had it cut?"

"About three months ago."

"You do have a job, don't you?"

"Of course I do."

"And nobody minds that crazy hair of yours?"

"Nobody has ever said anything about it. Is it that bad?"

"Like a lion just waking up."

"Ooh, that's bad."

"You must work in a really nice place."

She was right.

A St. Bernard trumps a waking lion.

What she had said, though, was not "Go to the barber," but rather, "Shall I cut your hair?" As a matter of fact, for a very long time she had been the one who cut my hair, and Yuji's. Could it be that somewhere inside her she remembered that?

"You'll cut it for me?" I asked.

She nodded. "It seems like something I'd be able to do."

"You've been cutting my hair for a long time."

"Then everything will be okay."

They say the hands remember.

In the end, it wasn't so okay. I'll write about that later.

She fixed breakfast and lunch, which allowed me to spend the morning relaxing, for the first time in ages. I drank the herb tea she made and told her about herself, as the thoughts came to me.

Where had those tea leaves been hiding, I wondered.

Your birthday is January 18th. That makes you a Capricorn, which every form of astrology known to man says makes you cautious and patient. Before we got married, your maiden name was Enokida. The house you grew up in is in a town thirty minutes north of here by train. Your father and mother, and your sister and brother, still live there.

You do not resemble anyone else in your family. Ever since you were born you have always looked more like a member of my extended family.

My parents live in a town about fifteen minutes south of here by train.

I have no brothers or sisters. I am an only child, of whom people say, "That itself is a sickness."

I actually have plenty of problems, not just that, but we can save that discussion for later.

When you were in junior high, you were in the gymnastics club. You were particularly good on the horse vault. I saw you perform one day and your jumping power was very impressive. Compared to you, the other club members looked like babies stamping their feet.

You, though, had a problem with sticking the landing, so your scores were always around 6.5. The group accepted you as a member, even though you were a little bit of a klutz. So in high school you made a good choice by switching from apparatus gymnastics to rhythmic gymnastics. In rhythmic gymnastics, after a big jump you can keep moving, and you don't have to land in place.

"I did rhythmic gymnastics?"

"Yes, you did. Your club was very well known. You won lots of awards in league competition."

"Wow!"

"You yourself were a very successful athlete. You didn't compete at a national level, but in regional competitions you did very well."

"I can't believe it."

"Why not?"

"I mean, rhythmic gymnastics, right?"

"That's right, rhythmic gymnastics."

"Me?"

"Yes, you."

Mio chuckled.

"This is strange."

"I'm sure it is."

"How about you?" Mio asked. "Were you in a club?"

"I ran track and field."

"You were a runner."

"I still run. In high school I ran the 800 meters."

Mio said, "Wow," and wrinkled her nose. "That sounds painful."

"No matter how painful it was…" I began. "It was something I chose for myself, so it didn't seem that painful."

"Really?"

"I'm positive."

*"Yo, Yuji!"*

From the next room came an overly familiar male voice. Mio was startled, and her body stiffened.

"It's just the alarm clock," I said. "Listen!"

*"Hey there, look! I brought you a present."*

*"Look! Here it is! Open your eyes and take a look!"*

*"That's right, open your eyes a little more! Here it is, here!"*

"Where?" We could hear Yuji's little voice.

*"Here it is! That's right! Open your eyes!"*

"So, where is it?" This time Yuji's voice was much clearer.

*"That's good! Now your eyes are open. Take a good look. This is the best present you could ever have. A new day!"*

"Aargh! Fooled again!"

"Good morning," Yuji said as he emerged from the next room, rubbing his eyes.

"My boy needs a haircut even more than you do."

"Oh, that's just bed-head. It's pretty bad every morning. I don't know how he sleeps…"

Yuji's head looked just like Woodstock, the cute little yellow bird from *Peanuts*. Like some wanderer who is always walking straight into the north wind. He was wearing a pajama top and underwear whose elastic was getting loose. He had left his pajama bottoms in the futon.

He looked at us with eyes that were not yet focusing. He scratched his head lightly. He was thinking about something.

He closed his eyes and opened them again slowly.

"Mom?" Yuji's face grew rapidly redder, and tears came to his eyes. "Mom, it's you, right?" He rushed to Mio and grabbed her arm. "It's Mom. She's come back!"

He put his arms around her waist and pressed his cheek to her chest. "Mom, Mom," he said over and over, and he squeezed Mio with all his strength.

I got up from my chair and stood behind him.

His droopy underwear looked just like a diaper. His two legs emerging from them were painfully thin, and his blue veins were clearly visible on the backs of his thighs.

"Yuji," I said. "Mom was sick but now she's getting better. Look, she made breakfast for us. She never went away, so don't make such a fuss."

Yuji's shoulders fluttered, and he held his breath for a minute, thinking. Somewhere in his little head, he was working hard to bring back everything that had happened since yesterday.

"Mom hit her head and lost her memory. Remember?"

Still clinging tightly to Mio, Yuji nodded his head.

"You're a crybaby, aren't you, Yuji?"

Yuji nodded again.

"So, let's eat. Mom made it for us. It looks delicious."

Yuji slowly let go of Mio, and with his head still bent, sat down in his chair.

"First go wash your face and brush your teeth."

Still looking down, he went into the bathroom. I followed him with my eyes and then returned my gaze to Mio.

"As I said yesterday, Yuji's an awful crybaby."

"It seems so."

"He was just so happy to wake up and see you standing there for the first time in such a long time. Until yesterday morning you couldn't get out of bed."

"Really?"

She turned that somewhat puzzled look on me again. A stiff smile came to my face, as if to say, "What do you mean by that look?"

"There is something strange going on here," Mio said.

"What do you mean?"

"The two of you."

"Nah," I said. "Not particularly. There's nothing strange about us."

My little sham was nearing the breaking point. I felt like some two-bit actor, whistling to cover the fact that I was lying.

Yuji came back and sat down again.

"Let's eat! Dig in!" I said loudly, to steer the conversation back from the brink.

"I'm starving!" Yuji chimed in.

For a while, Mio just looked at us, first one, then the other, but we pretended to be busy eating and not noticing.

Finally she let out a sigh, and said, "The two of you should eat a little more carefully. You're spilling food all over the place."

When breakfast was over, I took off my pajamas and changed for work. Seeing me all dressed up, Mio gulped. Thinking I looked really different to her somehow, I struck a pose like some model in *GQ* magazine.

"Takkun," Mio said.

"What is it?"

"You wear that suit to work?"

From the way she spoke, I realized I had misread her expression.

"Well, yeah," I said.

"That's a winter suit, isn't it? The material is really thick and heavy, for cold weather."

"You think so?" I said, sounding just like Yuji.

"And, it's not the right size for you. The jacket definitely needs some tailoring."

I never realized.

Nobody had ever told me.

Suddenly, like a revelation, I remembered Ms. Nagase in my office and her strange attitude.

That was it. This was what she had been trying to tell me all along.

"I guess I've lost weight. Quite a bit," I said, by way of explanation.

When Mio died, I could hardly eat a thing. I had never been a big eater, and I started eating even less, and before I knew it I was very thin. My weight dropped from 136 pounds to 119 pounds. At that point, it leveled off.

No wonder my suit looked big.

I had no time to think about things like that.

All I did was grab the nearest suit hanging in the closet, and I just kept wearing it.

Mio looked in the closet and found a suit that was lighter, more appropriate for warm weather, and handed it to me. I tried it on, but it was also too big.

"This is very strange," she said, looking at me, in my droopy-shouldered suit, with my stupid grin on my face.

"What is?"

"Do you really live here?" This time her glance was tinged with pity.

"I believe I am your wife, but could it be that this is really some stranger's apartment, and we've just barged in here for some reason?"

A very understandable conclusion. That would also explain

to her why the apartment was so dirty. Because we don't actually live here.

It would explain why the suits don't fit me. They must be somebody else's suits.

"No, that's not the case," I said. "This is our apartment. As I said before, I've just lost a lot of weight."

"How come?"

"Oh, well, that's just one of my many problems. Someday you'll understand."

"Someday? When will that be?"

She crossed her arms. Her face seemed to say, "I'm not giving another inch."

"Tonight," I said. "Tonight I'll tell you. About all my problems."

"Okay then. I'm looking forward to it." At that, Mio turned to help Yuji with his morning preparations. He had been buttoning his own buttons for a long time, but she even did that for him. It was a regression.

Oh, who cares.

Watching them, I felt this whole apartment had gone back more than a year in time.

Before leaving, I said to Mio, "You should try not to go out if you can."

She didn't seem to make too much of that, and nodded lightly.

"You're still pale. You should take it easy at home."

"Don't worry, I will."

What I was worried about of course was not her, but the people in our neighborhood. We were not overly friendly with our neighbors, but still, more than a few people were aware that Mio had died a year ago.

This apartment building is not quite typical. Of the six units, four are single rooms, and only the two units at the east end of the first and second floors (our place) have two rooms. For that reason, most of the people in the building were students or professionals living alone. Three units had turned over in the past year, but a few people would still know about Mio: the man in 101, just below us, and the young couple in 103. Everybody goes to work in the daytime, so I wasn't worried that if Mio went out she would run into them, but still it made sense to err on the side of caution.

From the front door Mio watched Yuji and me as we left.

"See you later!"

Memory or no memory, people are accustomed to dealing with the world in certain ways. Just now, the way she stood in the door seeing us off, her voice, the expression on her face, were all exactly as they were when Mio was alive.

"See you later, Yuji!"

She stopped herself from adding "kun," and she smiled a big smile.

Next she turned to me and said, "See you later!" and then she seemed to grow pensive again.

"That reminds me," she said. "I don't think I know your name."

I nodded and told her my name. "It's Takumi."

"Takumi?"

"That's right. It means 'good with his hands.'"

"Oh, I see. Takumi-san."

"Not that I'm actually good with my hands at all. Just the opposite in fact, despite my name."

"So I see," she said with a quick smile, "That's why they call you Takkun."

"That's right."

Yuji and I set off once more, and Mio said again, "See you

later, Takumi."

People might say I'm in love, but I had never before felt a pain in my chest like this one.

I felt like I was about to cry.

Surely we had said these same words a thousand times before. Every morning, these were the words she used to send me off to work. These words themselves said everything there was to say about our married life.

"See you soon," I said, lovingly.

In all these simple expressions—"Good morning," "Good night," "Looks delicious," "Are you okay?" "Did you sleep well?"—that's where love lives.

That's what it means to be a couple, I thought.

At that time I didn't realize it though.

# 8.

When I got to the office, the first thing I did was say to Ms. Nagase, "Sorry I'm late, but I had to change my suit."

I brushed my hands along my body, to show her my nice summer-weight suit.

"Ah, so I see." For some reason she blushed and started to fidget. I thought she would be happy, but she seemed more like a child flustered about some nonsense or other.

"That's what you were worried about all this time, wasn't it."

"Well, yes, but…" Her face grew redder and redder.

"I'm sorry you were so worried about me."

At this, she held her hands in front of her chest and shook them, as if to say, "No, not at all," and then she ran into the kitchenette.

She is a very unusual woman, I thought.

I did my work more carefully than usual. I wrote more notes, because I decided to write down even the littlest thing, even things I wouldn't usually write down, as messages to myself. My clipboard was soon covered with these missives to the me of ten minutes from now. That was because, underneath, I was so thoroughly lacking in reliability. My head was filled with thoughts of Mio.

It was just like falling in love. That is to say, based on my own meager experience, this was exactly like falling in love.

"A-ha!" I thought.

This is love.

I am in love.

I am in love with my wife's ghost.

Fantastic.

At the same time, this made me feel uneasy. All I could think about was that she might go away again. The premonition of that loss, combined with the feeling of love, suffused my chest with chemicals attached to words like "heartrending" and "endearment." All the while nursing an urge to fly home right away, just to see her face, somehow or other I managed to get through my work for the day.

"Just like," was all I could think. Just like a teenager in love for the very first time.

More than likely, most people fall in love over and over again with the same partner. And each time, they turn back into a teenaged child, complete with pimples and an overly sensitive heart.

# 9.

"I'm home," I said, short of breath, as I entered the apartment.

"Welcome home," said Mio and Yuji, their voices joining in a warm chord. I breathed a sigh of relief.

Their two voices were remarkably similar. In fact, my voice and Yuji's were also similar. My voice and Mio's, though, were completely different.

It's very strange.

Mio was cutting Yuji's hair.

Yuji was sitting in a chair, and Mio was casually chopping away at his hair with scissors.

This was a familiar and nostalgic scene. The plastic sheet

spread out on the *tatami* was also the same as always.

"Takkun," said Yuji. "Mom is cutting my hair."

"So I see."

I took off my suit jacket and hung it on a hanger in the closet.

"Huh?" I said. "The apartment is all tidied up!"

"Really?" said Yuji.

"It was a lot of work," said Mio.

"You didn't have to go to all that trouble. You're still not well."

"I just couldn't stand it. I mean, speaking as a model housewife."

"Well, I can see it was a lot of work."

"No more than you'd expect," Mio said.

I was very happy. More than the fact that she had cleaned the apartment, it was just that it was so in character for her. She actually was very nearly a perfect housewife. Even without her memory, Mio was unmistakably herself. That was what made me so very happy.

"Well then, how's that?"

Mio looked at me with an awkward smile. I got a bad feeling.

"Let's see," I said as I approached Yuji to check out his haircut.

"Well?" Yuji asked. "Do I look good?"

There was quite a gulf between the look on my face and the words I spoke. "Yeah, you look great."

Yuji's bangs carved an irregular arch quite high on his forehead. On the right his hair was cut too short, so you could see his scalp in two places. In the back there was one more place where his pink scalp showed through, and the hairline was much higher than it should have been. He looked like a punk rocker wearing a wool cap.

The truth is, he looked like an idiot.

"Well, I said the hands would remember," I said, prompting Yuji to say, uneasily, "What?"

"Hmm. I guess people can forget this sort of thing too," Mio said.

"What?" Yuji asked again, his voice a little louder this time.

"Okay, Takkun, you're next." My face must have shown my apprehension because Mio sounded pretty unnerved as she continued. "Don't worry. I think I got the hang of it from cutting Yuji's hair."

Yuji said, "What do you mean?"

And so, I sat down where Yuji had been.

Liberated, Yuji ran to the bathroom.

"Ugh," we heard him say, and then all was quiet.


"Okay then, I'm ready," I said, casting a sidelong glance at the bathroom.

"Try not to fidget," Mio said. "I don't want to cut anything but hair."

Hearing those words, my already frightened heart could feel my whole body cringe.

"Your hair is really curly," Mio said.

"When I was a kid, everybody called me Temple."

"Temple?"

"Like Shirley Temple. You know, from *The Little Princess*."

"No, I don't. Maybe I just forgot."

"Well, she was just a kid in a movie from fifty years ago."

She smiled as if to say, "No way I'd remember something like that."

The truth is, I had asked her the same thing before and gotten the same smile.

So, in 2050, I'm going to ask her, "Do you know Victoire Thivisol?"

Needless to say, she is the child star of *Ponette*. The first time we had this conversation it gave me a hazy sense that we would still be together in 2050. Even if we would both be old and tired.

Just one smiling vignette from the time when we were happy.

"Okay, all done."

This time she was full of confidence.

Fearfully I looked into the mirror she held. I could see the face of a worried man looking back at me. That man's haircut was a bit odd but still presentable. Something like a benevolent Sid Vicious. Come to think of it, he too is now a resident of Archive.

"All right," I said.

"It seems I got the hang of it this time. This is not bad."

"What about me?" Yuji asked.

He was wearing his yellow school cap.

"No problem. You look really cute. Nobody could help but love you," I said.

"Really?"

"Really. Right?"

Mio looked as though she didn't know what to say.

"Please forgive me, Yuji," she said. "But what Dad said is true. I didn't make you look too sharp, but nobody could help but love you."

"You too, Mom?"

"Of course. Just looking at you my heart beats faster."

"Well okay then," Yuji said, removing his cap. Even before his haircut, his amber hair, all plastered down, looked just like a knitted cap.

He really was cute though. That's the strange thing about children. They use the magic of reversal, turning faults into charms. Even if that is a kind of magic that only really works on parents.

Told to take a bath while dinner was being prepared, Yuji and I headed for the tub together.

"But Mom, you used to be so good," Yuji said, taking off his clothes.

"Good?"

"At cutting hair."

"Oh, well. I guess I forgot, even something like that."

"Really?"

"I guess so."

"But you remember how to cook."

"Now that you mention it, that seems to be the case."

It was true.

I wonder how that choice is made, how memories are kept or lost? I wonder if somehow it was more important to her to remember recipes than to remember about Yuji and me?

That would mean that Yuji and I were thinner gruel than rice omelets or cream stew.

I couldn't stand that. There must be some other reason.

That's what I choose to believe.


As I washed Yuji's hair I asked him, "Are you happy Mom is here again?"

After thinking a while, he said, "I'm not sure."

That was not what I was expecting to hear, and I was a bit shocked.

"Why wouldn't you be happy?"

"Well," Yuji said, wiping shampoo from his forehead, "Mom lives on Archavie, now, doesn't she?"

"That's right."

"So, someday she'll have to go back there again."

"But listen, Mom seems to have forgotten that too."

Yuji shook his head slowly. "Even if Mom has forgotten, somebody will come get her. That's the way all the stories go. In

94

the end, everybody goes back where they came from," he said. "It makes me want to cry."

Even so Yuji, still just a child, understood. If you think of someone you love, that thought is inseparably intertwined with the premonition of parting. He had already learned that once.

"Even so," I said. "Right now she is here with us, and we should be happy about that. We have to cherish this time we have together."

Yuji said "Yeah," but I couldn't tell what he was really thinking. I held the shower nozzle over his head and said, "I just want to make sure you understand, your mom was with us for a long time. Before she ever left us."

"I know," he said. "But something's strange about her now."

"That's true. So we have to be even more careful."

"Got it."

"Okay. You can go now."

Leaving the bathroom, Yuji shouted, "Mom, I'm out now! Dry me off!"

"Well done," I thought. After a year of having me tell him how to do things for himself, he lost no time reverting to his old childish ways.

When I emerged from the bathroom, Yuji was wearing nothing but baggy white kid's underpants, and Mio was cleaning his ears. She was kneeling, with his head on her thigh. His eyes were closed, and he had a happy smile on his face.

"This is pretty incredible," she said. "Just look what's in his ears! Have you been cleaning them?"

"I haven't," I said. "I just assumed he was taking care of it himself."

"You can't expect a six-year-old child to do that." She mumbled a little. "What's this?" and "What is going on here?" But then, all of a sudden, she fell silent, the words stuck in her throat.

After that, there was a dry sound as something struck the table.

"Takumi-san," she called to me. "Come here."

Still rubbing my wet head with a bath towel, I walked over to them.

"What is it?" I asked.

She was pointing to something on the table, and I leaned my face down to squint at the object.

It looked something like a black snail shell. I picked it up in my hand. It had a hard surface.

"Could this be...?" I began fearfully. "Was this in Yuji's ear?"

Mio nodded and made a face as if she had put something bitter in her mouth.

"Wah!" I said, and threw the snail-thing across the room.

"Wah!" echoed Yuji. "Takkun, don't yell so loud! You're hurting my ears!"

He covered his ears with his little hands.

Only then did I understand.

That's why he was always saying "Huh?" and "What?" All because of the layers and layers of petrified crud in his ears. He had carefully preserved a whole year's worth of earwax in those tiny little holes. He always did like to bury things. Like the bolts from the old factory.

From the hole in his other ear emerged a similar snail of hardened wax.

His hearing improved immediately, but he seemed to hate that.

For quite a while he complained, "Wow, what's that?" and "That's really strange," and "Don't be so loud!"

This is how, one by one, Mio retuned the tonic intervals that had gradually grown off-pitch over the past year. What does it mean that she, who had no memory, and who was perhaps not even really alive, was so much more grounded than I am? This just goes to show that she was something really special.

For Yuji and me, she was a woman of legend.

# 10.

After dinner, the three of us went for a walk.

Mio's head still hurt, but she hoped the evening breeze would help her forget about it. I had some reservations, but I decided it would be okay because in the dim of the evening all that people would see of us would be silhouettes.

We walked through a graded gouache landscape the color of thinned India ink. A wan moon hung over the treetops. On the surface of the water in the rice paddies, its reflection shimmered in the wind.

"It's a bit chilly tonight, isn't it," Mio said.

"That's because it's been raining."

Yuji and Mio, hand in hand, walked ahead, and I walked a bit behind them. I too had that simple desire to hold hands, but of course I was not able to say so. I was a bit envious of Yuji for doing so easily something of which I was incapable.

"So?" she asked. "Tell me about your many problems. You said you would tell me later, didn't you?"

"Uh...I guess I did."

The road came to a canal, and we turned left. I could see a railroad crossing blinking in the distance.

"Before that, though, I'd like to talk about the two of us a little more."

"Sure...fine."

I picked up my pace a bit to draw alongside her.

"When," I started. "When we were in high school we were not yet boyfriend and girlfriend."

"Because I was a terribly skinny, dull, short-haired model student with glasses, right?"

I smiled a little but did not turn to look at her.

"But," I said.

"Yes?"

"But, I happened to like terribly skinny, dull, short-haired model students with glasses."

"Really?" Yuji asked.

"It's true. It's just that, at that time, I didn't think that girls like that were looking for love."

"Looking for a partner in love?" Mio said.

"That's right. I misunderstood the signals."

"You mean me?" asked Mio. "What did I think of you then?"

"The same. I was a bit different from most people, and some people even said I was anti-social. Even you would never have thought of falling in love with someone like that."

"Did I say that?"

"You did."

"We were both late bloomers. We were always jumping to

conclusions like that."

"Yeah, we were world-class late bloomers," I said. "And on top of that, we were totally into our club activities. For you that meant jumping and spinning and throwing."

"Rhythmic gymnastics."

I nodded. "For me it was running around and around that 400-meter oval track."

"Was that fun?"

"It was fun. It's such a universal activity. I mean, even electrons and planets go around and around, around and around."

"Is that what it's like?"

"Yes it is."

We came upon the little railroad crossing. The road continued along the canal and disappeared in the distance.

Mio squinted hard at the road ahead, wrapped in darkness.

"Everything looks a little fuzzy to me," she said.

"Is that so?"

"Don't I wear glasses anymore?"

"Ah," I said. "No."

I had completely forgotten about that. Ordinarily, Mio wore contact lenses. Sometimes she wore glasses at home, but she almost never relied on her eyes alone. Her eyesight was pretty bad.

I lied to her.

"You haven't been wearing glasses lately. I mean, you don't have to look at any blackboards anymore, and you don't drive a car."

"But, I'm having trouble seeing. I must have glasses. Right?"

"I'm not sure where they might be. I'll have a look for them."

"Please do."

It seems contact lenses aren't supplied on Archive.

"At any rate," I said, trying to get the conversation back on track. "Since we were both late bloomers, less than five-year-olds, we ended our high school years with no experience in love."

"Even more of a late bloomer than me?" Yuji asked.

"I wonder," I said. "Maybe so."

"What's a late bloomer?"

"It means someone who matures slowly."

"Ha!" Yuji yelled. "You were really slow!"

Mio and I looked at each other and chuckled.

I said to her, "The thing that changed our relationship was a very small event on graduation day."

Graduation day.

We were not thinking at all that we might never see each other again, but really there was no reason we should ever see each other again. That's what partings are usually like.

But something happened that changed all that.

After the graduation ceremony was over, after we went back to our classrooms, after the last homeroom meeting of our high school years, after all of that was really over, that's when it happened.

I took some cartoon character items out of my desk (fast-food discount coupons, figurines from snack boxes, special ice-cream sticks, things like that) and was stuffing them into my sports bag, when from the desk next to mine you said, "Aio!"

"What is it, Enokida?"

"I want you to write something in this." And with that, you thrust a book in front of me. On graduation day, all the students were passing these books back and forth for each other to sign. But you were the only one who asked me. Who besides you would have asked me?

"Okay," I said. "Hand it to me."

I took the book from you, thought a bit, and wrote these

words: *It was nice sitting next to you. Thanks.*

That was my thanks for all the notes you had ever lent me, and my response to all the chemicals I had ever unconsciously received from you.

Your response to these words was, "I also thought it was nice to sit next to you. Thanks."

And we went our separate ways.

"Well, then. Goodbye."

"Yeah. Goodbye."

I picked up my bag, with my diploma and my cartoon characters, and left the room.

"You mean, nothing happened at all."

"No, something happened."

About a month after graduation, a letter from you arrived.

*I have your mechanical pencil. What should I do with it?*

"Ah, that's where it is!" I yelled.

For a whole month I had been looking for that pencil. When I handed back your signature book, my pencil was stuck in the pages, but I didn't remember until your letter came. Of course I hadn't been able to find it by looking in the street.

If it had been any ordinary mechanical pencil I wouldn't have made such a fuss, but this was not any ordinary mechanical pencil. My favorite aunt had bought it for me, my mother's sister, who was very dear to me.

I think everyone has this experience. The first time somebody buys something like that for them, they really love it like it's something special. A first book, a first watch, a first CD. I always took special care of those things.

I wrote back to you right away.

*The pencil is important to me. I'll come get it.*

I thought it would be wrong to put you to the time and

expense of sending it, so I decided to go get it myself.

You wrote back: *I'm at the dorm now. I will contact you when I'm home again.*

The return of the mechanical pencil was postponed until the following summer vacation.

I knew where it was, so there was no need to hurry. My small wish was also to see what had become of you as a college student.

We were both in college and continuing our club activities, so our schedules were packed with meets and overnights, and it was hard for us to get together. It was September 7th, nearly the end of summer vacation, before we were actually able to arrange a meeting. I remember exactly because it was Labor Day. I had memorized all the U.S. national holidays.

We arranged to meet in the concourse of a train station midway between your house and my house. I arrived five minutes early, but you were already there.

Finding you waiting there amid the throngs of people, I had a strange feeling, difficult to describe. Until that point I had not even realized such a feeling existed. Needless to say, it was love.

I may have been a late bloomer, but at that moment I was finally grown up.

Banzai!

At first I thought I was simply glad to see you again after such a long time. It really was very nostalgic.

We had spent three years never more than six feet apart, and you had left a piece of yourself in a very personal place within me, very close to the place where my father, or mother, or favorite aunt were. I could tell that the piece of you inside me was very happy to see you again.

You had prepared a small surprise for me. It made my heart pound, and I was dancing on air.

"A surprise?"

"That's right."

"What kind of surprise?"

"Well, let me tell you."


You had let your hair grow to your shoulders.

All through high school your hair had been very short. Now it was a bit longer. Your bangs came to about the middle of your eyebrows, and the hair from the sides of your head was bound in the back with a barrette. You had switched from eyeglasses to contact lenses, but I had already seen you that way in high school. So for me that day the happiest surprise was seeing your hair long.

It made you seem really feminine. Not the spirit of a coffee spoon anymore, but a real girl, of the right age to have warm skin and that really wonderful scent.

You didn't say anything like "I have no interest in boys, so leave me alone." I felt as though you were saying to me, *"Look at me, and fall in love with me."*

I was a simple sort, kind of gullible, taking whatever was right in front of my eyes at face value, and I simply accepted the signals you were emitting.

*"I understand. I will love you."*


I noticed that your smile seemed awkward. I think you were nervous too. For both of us it was the first time we had a date with a member of the opposite sex.

"Hi. It's been a long time," you said.

"Yeah, it sure has."

And then, neither of us knew what to say next. I thought for a while, and then I said, "Miss Enokida, is that Mr. Aio next to you?"

You got it right away. You said, "No. It's Mr. Teddy Bear."

We both laughed.

Once when I had cut class in high school, someone had put a stuffed teddy bear in my seat. We were remembering the conversation you had had with the teacher.

At that moment, I was in the track room by myself, reading Alan Sillitoe's *Saturday Night and Sunday Morning*.

In the end, the teacher said to you, "I thought so. The hair is too thick for him."

There is more to this story.

The next day, Mickey Mouse was sitting in my seat. Again the teacher asked you the same question, and you gave the same type of answer.

At that, she said, "I thought so. The ears are too big for him."

That day too, I was in the track room, reading more of the same book.

This little game became very popular. Without my knowing it, lots of stuffed animals took their turn in my seat. Winnie the Pooh, Snoopy, Donald Duck. They were said to be too fat, too white, their mouths too big, to be me.

You always answered seriously, which was great, and the teacher always came up with a fresh comment, which was also great.

Later, when you told me about all this, I felt sorry. I wanted to have been there, to hear the dialogue between you and the teacher.

At any rate, for the two of us it was a familiar episode.

We relaxed and eventually remembered why we had arranged to meet like this.

"So," you said.

"Mechanical pencil, right?"

"That's right. Mechanical pencil."

From your tote bag, which had a hibiscus pattern, you took an envelope.

"Here you are," you said, and handed it to me. "I noticed right away that day, but you were already gone."

"Yeah."

"And then I was so busy getting ready to move into the dormitory that I never had time to call you. I'm so sorry."

"Not at all. It was my mistake," I said. "And now I have it back."

I took the pencil out of the envelope and held it up to the light. "It was a birthday present from my aunt. It was the first mechanical pencil anyone ever bought me."

"When was that?"

"My tenth birthday. She bought it at the Kichijoji Station building."

"Ah. When you were in Tokyo."

"That's right."

Before moving to this town I had lived in the Chofu section of Tokyo. At that time, you lived in Minami-Azabu, in Minato-ku, also in Tokyo. At some point we might have been looking up at the very same clouds.

We were that close.

"Thank you very much," I said.

"Not at all. Don't mention it," you said.

The problem was, we had now completed our business. There would have been nothing unusual if we had simply parted at this point.

But we didn't want to.

Standing there in the milling crowd, looking at each other's faces, we were each waiting for the other's next words. I was hoping you would do something, and I noticed you seemed to be expecting the same thing from me.

At this rate, things would be over in a minute.

I ventured a "Well, then..." You looked at me with eyes that suggested you were eagerly awaiting something. I took courage from that look and continued talking.

"Are you thirsty?" I said.

"It is hot," you said. You were really thirsty. You nodded your head twice.

"Let's go find something cold to drink."

And the two of us set out to find the venue for our very first date.


When we reached the railroad crossing we decided to turn back.

"How's your headache?" I asked Mio.

"Mmm, it seems to be a little better, thanks."

"That's good."

Yuji said he was getting sleepy, and I picked him up and carried him on my back. Soon I could hear the familiar thick breathing of his sleep.

I wonder if he has sinus congestion.

"He looks cute when he's sleeping," Mio said.

"He looks just like you. Especially when he's sleeping."

"Maybe so. Somehow it really reminds me of old times."

"You mean when you were a child?"

"Yeah. Not that I can actually remember anything. But it's like that feeling."

"You still don't remember anything?"

"Not a thing. But I am feeling more clearly that I am your wife, and Yuji's mother."

"Doesn't that bother you? That you have no memory?"

"It's irritating, but it's not something to get too upset about. It's a matter of patience, I think."

"Well then, that's fine."

Mio kicked a pebble at the side of the road. It was an old habit of hers. Even without her memory, unconscious actions like that don't change.

"I was…" Mio said, "…happy, wasn't I?"

"You think so?"

"I do. I was together with the first person I ever loved, I had this beautiful boy, and even now we are still living happily together."

"Yeah. Sure."

I wonder if you were happy.

I asked myself, deep down in my heart.

Married to a man like me, with all my problems, never having traveled anywhere, living out your short life in this little town. Can anybody really call that happy?

"How about you?" Mio asked. "Are you happy? Do I make you happy?"

"I am happy," I said. "Very."

I had been a penguin flying through the sky.

Higher than I had ever dreamed of, I climbed, following her lead.

Close to the stars.

From there, the dirty things on Earth, the ugly things, all the things that make the heart suffer, looked like a beautiful tapestry.

That was happiness.

Then she left, and I was just a penguin. Sadness had visited, but I had the memory of the sky, and she had left me a boy who was a lot like her, with her wings that could cut through the wind.

In other words, I was a moderately happy penguin who was

occasionally attacked by sadness.

"Tell me what comes next?" she asked.

The three of us were lying side by side on the futons at home, looking at the ceiling bathed in pale orange light.

"Sure," I said. "I'll tell you the story until you fall asleep."

The truth was, though, I had almost entirely forgotten all about the events of that time. Mio had told me about them later many times, and I had come to accept these stories as my own memories.

This was becoming a strange tale indeed.

What I had forgotten and Mio had told to me I was now telling to Mio who had forgotten. It was like a two-person game of telephone. Through endless repetition, these memories had grown much more beautiful and dramatic than the actual past, and they may eventually become as beautiful as dreams. Actually, that's true of most people's memories.

Anyway, the tale of our first date.

We went into a coffee shop right across the street from the station. I ordered ginger ale, and you ordered iced coffee.

After three years of sitting next to one another, or behind each other, this was the first time we had ever sat face to face.

It was also the first time I had ever looked so closely at your face. Your eyes were single-lidded, but for that they were very large. The bridge of your nose was prominent, and your lips were thin. And then your eyeteeth. Yours was a face that could make very different impressions on different viewers. For me, it was the kind of female face I had always liked, ever since I was a young child.

That's what love is like.

"Your hair is longer," I said.

"That's right. Everybody in the gymnastics club has the same hairstyle."

A high chignon. That's what you called it.

"You look really different somehow."

"Do I?"

"Yeah. More grown up."

"You too," you said.

"Yeah, you seem more like an adult."

"Did you get taller?" you asked.

"A little."

"How tall are you now?"

"About five foot seven. As a middle-distance runner, I'd like to be a lot taller."

"You look taller than that."

"That's because I'm wearing boots."

In high school, we had only ever met in the classroom, so we always had indoor shoes or slippers on our feet. My favorites were a pair of bowling shoes that had been left in the classroom.

These were bowling shoes with a history, having been "borrowed" by a teacher from a nearby bowling alley some years before. The heels and toes were indigo blue, and the sides were white. And they sported the number 61 in a reddish-purple hue. For three years I wore those shoes indoors at school.

That day was the first time we had ever met that I was wearing boots, or anything else with taller heels. It was also the first time I ever saw you wearing an apricot-colored dress, and it was the first time I saw you wearing lip gloss. It was also the first time I saw you with a full head of hair that moved when you turned your head, and it was also the first time I had this fidgety, restless feeling all around my heart just from talking to you.

It was so hard to think of anything for which it was not the first time that it seemed as if everything was for the first time.

We stayed in that coffee shop for five hours.
It seems hard to believe.
What the hell did we talk about?

We were each hoping to learn everything about one another.

We were both terribly serious people, so we felt that getting to know each other in this way was the way that love happened.

Knowing nothing, we would never be able to hold hands. Not knowing your parents' names I would have doubts about taking your arm in mine. Only once we knew everything about each other—shoe size, clothing size, how many months old we were when we first learned to walk, how many seconds we could hold our breath underwater—only then could love rise to the next step.

In wanting to learn more about each other, we were showing that we wanted the other to know us as we were. It may seem like a peculiar way of thinking, but this was the path we chose, to approach each other slowly.

Therefore, conversation was important. We talked for five hours without so much as touching each other's pinkie fingers. How many words would we have to exchange before we got married? I was eighteen years old, and you were the first girl I ever really dated, but already I was thinking of marriage. I thought that was what dating meant.

I was dimly aware it would take a long time before we built up to a kiss. I was not particularly anxious—I thought that since we were looking for a partner to share a whole life together, we would have plenty of time. At the very least, we had already taken three years from the time we first exchanged words until we had our first date. I was sure that within three more years we would exchange a first kiss.

That was how I thought.

In five hours of conversation, we got a little closer to that kiss.

If we kissed, I wondered, would those eyeteeth get in the way?

Looking at your lips, I suddenly had thoughts like that.

It started to get dark, and it was time to go home.

Looking back now, that was our first date. In other words, that was the first step toward what came next. At that time, though, I would never have had the confidence to know that. More than marriage, more than a kiss, my very next assignment was simply to make the next date.

We left the coffee shop and crossed to the station concourse, where we bought tickets. We didn't talk about when we would next see each other. We went through the gate and down to the platform. My train would come in five minutes, and yours two minutes after that. Even so, all I could do was rattle on about how Emperor penguins raise their young.

I cannot remember how the conversation got onto that track, but I knew an awful lot about Emperor penguins. Remind me to tell you later.

You seemed to be listening intently, but inside I was nervous. The train was coming. And then the train came.

"I'll…" I said. "I'll see you off, and then get on the next train."

And then your train came.

"I'll…" you said. "I'll be okay waiting for one more train."

You had to be home by six.

A university student with a six o'clock curfew! We would never be able to shoot off fireworks.

Trains came and went at seven-minute intervals, but the time passed before we knew it. I think even if we'd had thirty days it would have been the same. Most decisions are made in the final few seconds.

Your train came, the doors opened, and the people on the platform boarded. You followed the other passengers onto the train. You looked back and smiled at me.

Only then did I say, "Uh...when can I see you again?"

The bell rang, indicating that the train was about to leave, and you said, "I'll be going back to the dorm."

So as not to be drowned out by the clanging bell, you raised your voice: "I'll write you a letter."

And the doors closed.

"I see," I said to the train as it left the station.

It's all right—this isn't the end of it. Endings and beginnings are as different as exits and entrances. At the entrance, you always have the feeling that there is definitely something there, just on the other side. Something really special, for sure.

At that time, that is how I thought.


Your letter arrived a week later. I wrote an answer the next day and mailed it. About a week after that, another letter arrived from you. This time I waited three days before answering.

This was our tempo.

A more passionate person might find this slow, but for us it was a very comfortable pace. We were two plain, serious, late-blooming people, and our love deepened quietly, slowly, and in moderation. It is possible, in this hectic world, that that was a great luxury.


The dormitory where you lived in Setagaya had only one telephone, but after curfew no one was allowed to leave their rooms to use it. Mobile phones did not yet exist, and even if they did, they were not something that you or I would have used.

We both hated the telephone.

The telephone was rude, arrogant, and pushy. And it often

connected us to rude, arrogant, and pushy people. Salesmen, people urging you to vote their way, friends you weren't that close to asking you to do favors for other people. Telephones and people like that seemed to have a lot in common.

The first words ever spoken on the telephone were arrogant.

"Mr. Watson, come here!" Those were Alexander Graham Bell's words, of course.

This foreshadows the subsequent development of the telephone.

At any rate, we preferred to exchange messages, not by telephone, but by mail.

Your handwriting was beautiful. Your pretty penmanship actually hinted you were a good student, thin, tall, with a voice that quavered a bit at the end of words.

It made me a bit ashamed. My handwriting was unbelievably bad.

If you will allow me to make excuses for a minute, it was all because of my parents' stubborn preconceptions. When I was a young child, my parents had forced me not to write with my left hand. They believed some pseudo-scientific statistics showing that left-handed people die young, and for a time they actually immobilized my left hand with string. I had no choice but to learn to use my relatively clumsy right hand to hold chopsticks, throw a ball, and to write. My bound left hand grew sulky and timid, and lost its ability to function smoothly. Now I write equally badly with either hand.

I think you probably have some of my letters among your possessions, but I wouldn't want you to look at them.

"Are there also letters I wrote to you here?" Mio asked.

"Yes, there are. I brought them here from my house when we got married."

"I'd love to read them. I wonder what they say."

"Just ordinary things, about your club practices, your dreams of the future."

"Dreams of the future."

"Yeah."

"When I graduated from college, I got a job, didn't I?"

"Yes, you did. You went to a two-year college, so you were twenty years old when you started working."

"What kind of job did I choose? Was it a dream job?"

"Yes, it was. You became the you you wanted to be."

"What was it? I really want to know. Tell me."

"You..." I said. "You were a dance instructor at a fitness club."

"Dance?"

"That's right. Aerobic dance."

"Me?"

"That's right. You."

"I can't believe it."

"Sure you can."

"But," I said. "You had done gymnastics in high school and college, and it really was a similar sort of thing."

"Ah, I see. Because of gymnastics."

"Yeah. You liked to dance. And you had always wanted to be a teacher. So you chose a profession where you could teach people the joys of dancing."

"Being an actual teacher seems like it would have been better though."

"You would have needed a teacher's certificate. In the end, you chose dance."

"So, I was an instructor until we got married?"

"Actually, until you got pregnant with Yuji. It was a while before you realized you were pregnant, so you continued working well into your pregnancy."

Mio gasped.

"My life!" she blurted out, staring at the ceiling bathed in orange light. "I don't know…"

"Huh?"

"I don't know. I feel like I tried to do too much. I can tell I really was just a quiet, serious student."

"Yeah."

"So, starting from there, the life I can imagine would have been a plainer, less difficult life."

"Ah. Maybe so."

"Don't you think? It's not a matter of liking or disliking. I could have chosen a job for its stability, or the company's good name, and worked as plain old office help, and just resigned myself to the fact that this was my life, and been satisfied and gone on living. That's what it looks like to me."

"I see."

"And never mind marrying for love, someone you really love. Arranged marriages are fine—marrying somebody because some relative's aunt owes somebody else a favor. That would have been my life and it would have been just fine. I would have been just as happy. I bet if I told you something like that you'd just keep nodding and saying, 'Yeah, sure.'"

"I understand," I said. "You always said things like that. 'I did the best I could, for me.' You always seem to take the safest route, but when you come to a narrow bridge with no handrail you shut your eyes and run across with all your might."

"Really?"

"Yeah. You were fantastic."

"Fantastic?"

"To have married someone like me. That decision was just incredible."

"But…"

"Listen, I said I would tell you later. About all my

problems."

"Yeah…"

"The life you chose, including all that, was not plain or trouble-free."

"Really?"

"That's right."

"Tell me more."

"To be continued…tomorrow."

"You're kidding, right?"

"Nope."

"You brought me this far…"

"Sure. It would take too long to tell the whole thing at once."

"But…"

"If I don't go to sleep soon I will be totally useless at work tomorrow. That's the only reason."

"But, it's only ten thirty."

"I've already stayed up too late for me."

"Really?"

"Yeah. So, good night."

"Good night."


"Are you really going to sleep?"

"Yes, I am."

"But…"

"Good night."


"Good night."


"Are you sure?"


"Huh?"

"That's just Yuji talking in his sleep. Don't worry about it. Good night."

"Good night."

"Are you sure?"

# 11.

Flying home from work on my bicycle, I noticed Nombre and Pooh ahead of me. As I pulled alongside them I got off my bicycle and said, "Nombre-sensei!"

Nombre paused before looking at me and said, "Oh."

Pauses like that were also a specialty of mine. Just as Mio always asked, "Where were you?"

"Heading home from work?"

"That's right."

"How's Yuji? Doing fine?"

"Yes he is. How about you?"

"Well, so-so. When people get to be my age it's always something or other. If your pain is five on a scale of ten you have to think you're doing all right."

"So, are you a five today?"

"Thereabouts."

Pooh was looking up at me, saying, "~?" I told him "Good doggie," and scratched his belly with my foot.

"How's your book coming along?" Nombre asked.

"Not so well. I've had to put it aside for a while."

Nombre said simply, "Oh? Now, why would that be?"

I sensed an impulse rising rapidly within me.

Should I tell him?

Should I tell him about Mio?

"Mio," I said simply.

Pooh said, "~?"

Nombre looked at me with the same face.

"She...?"

"Yes, she did."

"Yes, she did?"

"If I were to tell you she came back, what would you think?"

"Ah," he said, with a face full of conviction. "This is the story in your book, right? This is the situation, right?"

I nodded ambiguously and went on. "When she was alive, she said so. 'When the rainy season returns I will come to you.' To see how we're doing."

Nombre just listened, saying nothing.

"And she really came back. She was at that old ruined factory in the woods."

His face now looked a bit skeptical.

"And we brought her home, but she's lost her memory. She doesn't know who she is. She has even forgotten that she left this world a year ago."

"This is the story in your book, right?"

"No, this is real. She's in the apartment right now, waiting for me to come home."

"Mio is?"

"That's right, Mio is."

"In other words, you mean…"

"Her ghost," I said, finishing his sentence.

"And this isn't just the story in your book?"

"That's right."

He looked away from me and down at Pooh at his feet. Pooh looked up at him. They looked as though they were discussing whether to believe my story.

I decided to wait quietly until they came to a conclusion.

Mio had always liked Nombre.

When the two of us moved to this town as a couple, Nombre was the first person we ever really talked to. We were on our way home from buying some groceries for supper at the shopping center, and we met him in Park No. 17. That was seven years ago.

Even then he had seemed like a very old man—just like my boss at the office.

Pooh had been much younger, like a thoughtful, taciturn youth. Even then the only sound he could make was "~?"

Ever since then, a few times a week, we met in Park No. 17 for conversations that were neither too short nor too long, carrying on a friendship that was neither too shallow nor too deep. Both Mio and I were not especially good at talking to people, so this modest contact with this retired teacher was nearly our only social interaction. Nombre treated Mio like he would his own granddaughter, and she returned his affection.

And so,

And so, before the rainy season ended, I wanted to arrange for the two of them to meet again. Before she went back to Archive. The two of them.

Mio had surely forgotten all about Nombre, but if she were to meet him, there might be something that would pass between them. To accomplish this, I had to make sure Nombre was fully aware of the facts. If I just brought them together, his old heart might skip a beat, and he might just shut down completely.

"Well then," he said. "Mio…what is she like?"

He struggled to find the right words. He may have been trying to think of a euphemistic way of asking if she had legs.

"She's completely normal," I said. "She is the same old Mio. Her appearance, her personality, her voice, her scent. She just has no memory."

"Is that so?" He appeared somehow relieved to hear that.

"Would you like to see her?"

In response to my question, Nombre nodded a little, repeatedly. This was only a little different from his usual trembling, but I was sure it was a gesture of affirmation.

"So," I said. "How about tomorrow then. In Park No. 17."

"Same time as usual?"

"Sure. I'll bring her with me."

"Fine. I will be on my usual bench."

"Okay."

I said goodbye to Nombre and Pooh, got back on my bicycle, and headed for home again.

# 12.

Is it right to feel desire if one's wife is a ghost?

This is also a relativistic issue. In other words, I only felt that way because she was that way. By "that way," I mean even though she was a ghost she had a very healthy, seductive body. The same as those chemicals, this was an unspoken message directed at all of us males.

"Hey, look at me. Look at how ripe I am. I could have your baby any time."

Her rounded bosom, her narrow waist, that's what they were saying. Her spectacularly tight bottom says, *Leave it to me.*

But she was a ghost.

Ghosts cannot give birth to babies.

So, if that is the case, why does she look so hot?

I poured water in a glass and drank it. I could see Mio as she got out of the shower and began to dry off Yuji's body.

In our apartment, there's an area next to the sink where we undress for the bath. There is a vinyl screen, but we never pull it down. So I could see the two of them very clearly from where I stood.

She was without defenses, without a thing on her body, and she was drying Yuji with a towel.

I was seeing her body for the first time in a very long time. I remembered her as thin, but now I could see that while her breasts were small, they jiggled as she leaned over. And she had the backside of a dance instructor, well developed. "Leave it to me," it said.

Happy memories came back to me. Memories full of softness and heat.

I swallowed the water in my mouth.

She lifted her face and looked at me.

She was not particularly anxious, but slowly she raised the towel to cover herself. She looked straight at me the whole time, and I smiled shyly and walked away.

Later, she said to me, "Wait a minute."

"Huh?"

"I...I'm not ready yet, in my heart. I do have a real sense that I am your wife, but that..."

"Oh, you mean..."

"Yes, that."

"Not at all. Don't worry about it. Whatever you want is what I want. Whatever you don't want, I don't want it either."

"Really?"

"Really."

"But..." she said. "When you were looking at my body before, your eyes seemed to be saying you wanted me."

"Oh. I'm sorry. It was just a reflex, a response to a memory."
"A memory?"
"A memory of a while ago. Of your softness, your warmth."
The first half was a lie, the second half the truth.
"Really?"
Somehow, her gaze suggested she was dreaming.
"Did we...you know." She stammered a bit and then continued quickly, "Did we have a good relationship, you know, in that way?"
"That was, well..."
"What?"
"That was, well..."

That winter, we met on the first Monday after New Year's.
Our second date.

"It had been over three months since we'd seen each other, right?" Mio said, sitting across the table from me.
Yuji was listening intently to an Italian lesson on TV. He really liked the girl on that show.
"But we had sent lots of letters," I said. "It was as if we needed to exchange lots of words to get past a certain door. Then, on that day, the door just opened. I felt as if you had always been right there beside me.
"*Facciamo meta-meta!*" Yuji shouted.
"Huh?"
"It means, 'Let's share it half and half.'"
"Oh, I see."

This time we had again agreed to meet at the station concourse.
I remembered that when I had arrived five minutes early the last time you were already there, so this time I arrived fifteen

minutes early. Having ascertained that you were not there yet, I pulled a book from my Frank Shorter track bag and started to read. *The Sirens of Titan*, by Kurt Vonnegut (at that time he was still appending Jr. to his name). I was reading it for the third time. The past two times I had cried at the final scene. This time too, the tears were flowing. I was crying for Malachi Constant.

"Aio?" I raised my head and you were there. "Are you crying?" you asked.

"Yeah. I'm crying."

"What's so sad?"

I held up *The Sirens of Titan* and showed it to you. On the cover was a picture of the bones of a dog, with a collar and a leash.

"That's sad?"

I nodded.

For a long time after that, you thought it was a sad story about the death of a beloved dog.

I looked at my watch. It was still ten minutes before our agreed meeting time. We headed for our favorite coffee shop.

"Come to think of it," you said, "you always seem to be reading a book. Whenever you have a few minutes of down time, or study time, or whatever."

"Yeah, I guess so."

"I like books too. But I prefer things like *Sherlock Holmes* and *Arsene Lupin*."

"I know," I said.

"You do?"

I had been watching you more than you realized.

"That mohair sweater," I said. "It looks good on you."

"Thanks," you said.

We went into the shop and ordered. I pulled a package from my bag and set it on the table.

"Your birthday's coming up, isn't it?" I pushed the package

toward you. "Birthday present."

You made a very happy face. You looked from the present to me, and back again, and said you were happy.

"I've never gotten a present from a boy before. Thank you."

"Open it," I said.

The wrapping paper came from a year-end gift someone had given my father—some sweets, I think. When you opened your present, it gave off a vanilla scent.

"For me?" you asked.

"That's right, Miss Enokida."

It was a drawing, in pen, A4 size, in a cheap plastic frame. A drawing of you, from behind, that I had done with a steel pen and black ink. I was trying to remember something and draw it, and for whatever reason all I could think of was your back. I think I was happy that you had let your hair grow long.

Then, as now, my hair was really curly, and I always envied people with beautiful straight hair. This too must be a kind of fetishism, but much more biologically correct than a penchant for spike-heeled mules.

"I'm so happy. I'll put it in a special place."

When I think of this moment now, that such a cheap present made you so truly happy, I realize how important you were to me. The whole thing cost less than ¥1,000. Really serious students were often unbelievably poor. An elementary school girl would not have been as happy about this same present.

"You're very good at drawing pictures," you said.

"I wanted to go to art school."

"Why didn't you?"

"My eyes," I said. "They aren't very good. I have trouble distinguishing colors. To the point where I have trouble telling if the traffic light is red or green."

"I didn't know that."

"I didn't know it myself. I thought everybody saw the world

the same way I do."

"Really?"

"Yeah. But one of my teachers told me I should think of something else to be. He told me I would be better off as a regular company employee. It wouldn't give me any problems."

"What a waste," you said. "This drawing looks just like a photograph."

Even at that time, you were very good at building up my meager self-confidence. The important thing was that you weren't even aware of it yourself.

The simple words you tossed off without even thinking about them were very encouraging to me.

"I have a present for you too," you said. "Even though Christmas is over, and your birthday too."

It was a knitted headband.

"Your ears get cold when you run, don't they? So I thought..."

"Thank you," I said. "It's great."

I was indeed very happy.

And so,

I am still taking good care of it.

The headband.

Because it was the first present you ever gave me.

"On that day as well, you guessed it, we sat and talked for five hours."

"And the more words we exchanged, the closer we became to one another, right?"

"Yes, I'm sure."

"Really?"

"On that day, we actually held hands."

"That's fantastic!"

"I think so."

"We were really serious. That's terrific."

"Not so much, really."

As we waited for the train, you blew on your hands to warm them. Seeing you do that, I asked, "Are you cold?"

"Yeah. I lost my gloves. And I don't have any pockets."

There were no pockets on either your mohair sweater or your long checked skirt. I could tell that you were wearing several layers of clothing, but you were not wearing a coat or jacket over your sweater.

"I'll lend you my pocket."

You stood beside me and looked up at my face, and then you looked back down, and started blowing on your fingers again. There was a few seconds of silence, as if you were hesitating, and then you said, "Well, I don't mind if I do," and you put your left hand in the pocket of my pea coat. My right hand was already there, so of course our two hands touched. Your hand was really cold. Small and thin, your touch seemed really helpless. Without a second thought, I grasped your hand inside my pocket. Like a small, frightened animal, your fingers wiggled, and then gradually lost their strength.

"Just like a carnivore eating some poor animal that had entered its lair."

"That's right, I was eaten up."

"Thanks for the meal!"

When your left hand had warmed up, we changed positions, so you could warm your right hand.

"Welcome to my left pocket."

This was no longer the first time, so we were both more relaxed. This time it was your right hand meeting my left hand, but basically there was no difference from the first time. Exactly as anticipated.

"I had no hidden agenda."

"Apparently not."

"Hmm?"

"Yeah."

Mio smiled, a bit stiffly, turned to me and reached out her hand.

"Your hand please," she said. I reached out and touched her fingertips.

"Like this?"

"Yeah."

Gently she squeezed my hand.

"It's warm."

"Is it?"

"Like when we were eighteen," she said. "I'm getting to know you little by little. I like you."

For no reason at all (actually, there was plenty of reason), my heart started beating faster.

"Perhaps somewhere inside you remains some shred of a memory that you loved me."

"That's why..." she said. "That's why I can hold your hand like this."

She lowered her gaze and looked bashful.

"The fact that I can be bold this way is how I know I really am your wife. We fell in love, got married, and have spent years holding hands just like this. I bet we've even kissed."

"We have, haven't we?"

"Wait just a little more. I won't say you should wait three years. It's only been three days, and look, we're holding hands. Tomorrow we will know each other even better."

"I'm in no hurry," I said. "All I want is whatever you want."

"What I want is to get back to normal life, as soon as possible. As your wife, as Yuji's mom, I want to be able to do the things I'm supposed to do."

"You're already doing plenty."

"If that's the case," she replied, "then I want to be able to do even more. I want to able to be completely natural and relaxed."

"Did you know?" she asked.

"What's that?"

"My fingertips, intertwined with yours, are trembling."

"So it seems."

"It seems..." she said. "It seems as if I am holding hands with a man for the first time in my life. I'm all tensed up."

The truth is, it was very special for me too. Even if it didn't seem as long for me as it did for Mio, there had been a one-year blank in my life. I was holding my wife's hand for the first time in a year, and I too could not calm down.

Objectively speaking, it may seem ludicrous for a couple who spent six years together to get all red-faced just from holding hands. But for us this was a serious matter. It is also true that the more serious people are, the more ludicrous they sometimes seem.

*"Facciamo poco poco!"* we heard Yuji exclaim suddenly.

Surprised, we quickly let go of each other's hands.

"What is it this time?"

"It means, 'We should each take a little.'"

"Ah, is that so."

Mio was serious, but she was also a pragmatic woman. Rather than worry about this and that about having lost her memory, she was assessing the facts of the situation, and her plan was to do what she had to do, which was actually quite typical of her. Taking care of Yuji, doing the cooking, and all sorts of other things.

That was fine.

But...

She was a ghost.

At some point she would leave this world again. Seeing her go to all this trouble, unaware of that fact, was painful for me.

She didn't know.

That she had died a year ago. That before long, the time would come for her to leave us again.

# 13.

*Click!*

My eyes opened.

The clock by my pillow said 2:35. I was a little chilly. Outside the window I could hear the sound of rain.

At times like this, it was my habit to check on Yuji.

He was sound asleep, and I could hear the familiar sound of his breathing. His arms were up over his head—"Banzai!"—so I put them back under the blanket.

Mio was not there.

I got up from my futon and went into the kitchen. I found her by the sink sitting in a chair looking vacantly at her fingertips.

She noticed me and looked up.

"I'm sorry. Did I wake you?"

"No, not at all. There's this nasty guy, you see. He always switches off whatever dream I happen to be watching."

I pinched my thumb and middle finger together, to snap them, but the only sound they made is a slight rubbing. So I made the *Click!* sound with my mouth.

"At times like this," I said, "I can't go back to sleep right away."

"How about you?" I asked Mio, and slowly she turned to me.

"Sort of. I was thinking about a lot of things, and my eyes just won't stay closed."

So.

"It gets cold here."

At my urging, we moved into the kitchen and then into the room beyond. I beat the dust from a cushion and handed it to her.

"Here, take this."

"Thanks."

So we sat, side by side, each with our back in a big cushion, bathed in the soft light that came from the kitchen and from the bedroom next door.

"No need to hurry," I said. Without thinking about it, I lowered my voice to a whisper.

"*Poco poco.*"

"*Poco poco?*"

"One step at a time. Let's just take things one step at a time."

"That's right."

Outside I could hear soft drops of rain, and larger drops from the roof. These sounds seemed disciplined, orderly, never-ending. Mio was small and trembling, and she gasped as if she were freezing.

"Are you cold?"

"A little."

Gently, I put out my arm and wrapped it around her shoulder.

Through her cotton pajamas, I could feel her soft body.

"Thank you," she said. "Warm."

"That word," I said. "I haven't felt this way in a long time."

"Really?"

"Yeah. You used to say that same thing, the same way."

"When you would put your arm around me?"

"That's right. On very special nights."

"Have I heard about this yet?"

"No, not yet."

"Tell me. I want to know."

"Well then. I'll tell you."


It was a summer night, in the year we were twenty-one.

We met again for the first time in a year.


"Met again?"

"Yeah, until that time we were going our separate ways. We had broken up the summer before."

"We did?"

"That's right."

"Even though I was seeing you seriously?"

"That's right."

"I don't believe you."

"But it's the truth."

"What happened?"

"I told you already. I have a lot of problems."

"Yeah, you said you would tell me about them, but you haven't yet."

"I'm going to tell you now. It's the beginning of everything."

The beginning was very gentle, compared with the importance of what was to happen.

A slight fever that wouldn't go away. Not a cold, just a temperature of 100 degrees that went on and on.

Actually, I felt fine. Even off-season, my time in the 800-meter race was better than my previous personal best. My body was stronger than ever, and my mind was ready to take on the world.

At that time, I was not in the habit of eating very regularly. Even without eating, it seemed I drew limitless energy from the sun and the moon. I hardly needed to sleep either, and resting was more of a chore than a comfort. It was as if I had been struck by something that kept me in perpetual motion.

I practiced over six hours a day.

Without eating, without sleeping, between New Year's and summer I ran a total distance equal to a trip to the Marianas Islands.

And then...

The obvious result: I collapsed.


It was the second Saturday in April.

I had difficulty breathing, fell into a seizure, and was taken to the hospital. This was the very first time my internal switch had flipped—there was a *Click!*, a light went on, and the needle on my internal gauge maxed out.

Any time something happens for the very first time, you can't rely on your past experience, and everything feels out of proportion. I thought I was definitely going to die, and I became so afraid I thought my fear would kill me.

The upshot was this: I was diagnosed with pneumonia or maybe bronchitis. I was handed a pile of medicine bigger than my usual meal at that time, and I was sent home from the hospital. Three days later, though, I had another episode, and I was rushed back to the hospital. It was only much later that I realized this was all because of the flaw in the plans that were used to make me, which caused excessive amounts of powerful chemicals to be secreted in my brain.

I went around to several hospitals, and my little billfold filled with so many patient ID cards I could have done magic tricks with them. At each hospital I described my symptoms, at each hospital I gave a blood sample, and at each hospital the doctors scratched their heads.

The only conclusion I could come to was that no one knew what to think. This condition had many symptoms, but it had no name.

For many nights I could not sleep. I wanted to sleep, to escape my pain, and the fact that I could not sleep only added to my suffering.

Emerging from my room was a very difficult undertaking. At first I could not venture more than 600 feet from home (hospital visits didn't start until much later).

Seen from 300 feet away, my house looked like the sun seen from Pluto. At 600 feet away, I felt like an astronaut venturing outside the solar system, apprehensive, unable to stand there or move on. In the end, like a ball thrown up in the air, there was nothing for me to do but return where I had come from.

Of course I could not go to classes in this condition, and my future looked bleak.

We had agreed to a third date, but I wasn't able to make it. All I told you was that it was not convenient for me, and we promised to meet again in the summer.

"You didn't tell me you were sick?"

"No, I didn't. I don't know why—maybe because it didn't seem to be some ordinary sickness. It was a hard thing for me to say."

"You should have told me."

"You're absolutely right."

"Yeah."

"But at that time, I was about ready to give you up."

"Give me up?"

"That's right. It wasn't just that the future looked dim, I felt like I had no future. Or if I had one at all, I imagined depending on my parents to feed me and growing tomatoes in the garden, or something like that."

"But…"

"At that time, that was really what I was feeling. I didn't know what it was, but I knew something awful was happening to me. Something had changed, irreversibly.

"That's why," I said. "I could not bring myself to involve you with my life as it was. At that point we had done nothing more than hold hands. You could still back out."

I started to tell Mio about all the millions of problems that still plague me.

My memory is very, very bad.

"Short-term memory is particularly problematic for me. This seems to be because of something wrong with my hippocampus, in my brain. Hippocampus actually means walrus. Did you realize that every human being actually has a teeny tiny walrus in their brain? For whatever that's worth."

And then there are a lot of things I simply can't do. Ordinary things that ordinary people do all the time are just not ordinary to me.

Like leaving the house. At first I couldn't walk out my front door and go out more than 600 feet. But I tried and I tried, and slowly I increased that distance. I started taking a medicine that was relatively effective in treating my condition, and at one point I was able to go really quite far, but now a distance of about sixty-two miles is still my limit.

Of course, I don't have any way of traveling that far.

I can't take trains or buses. I can't take airplanes or submarines or spaceships. I can't even get on Star Tours at Disneyland. I cannot enter a movie theater, or any theater, or a concert hall.

I get worried a lot, and I feel much more anxiety than is appropriate or necessary, in all kinds of situations. From my perspective, I look at all the people living in this dangerous world of ours with ordinary expressions on their faces, and I think something must be wrong with them.

If I stopped breathing I would suffocate, but that doesn't worry me. Besides, forgetting to breathe would be a matter of supreme indifference.

Statistics show that hundreds of people die in traffic accidents every day. Walking around carelessly, blindly believing that you yourself will not be one of them is tantamount to a suicidal act. Letting go of a child's hand on the street is unforgivable negligence.

Allow me to say, though, that I am not like some drunk who thinks the building would collapse if he weren't holding it up.

"Really?"

"Don't you think?"

"I wonder…"

"Am I wrong?"

Who cares? I will admit, however, that I may be overreacting. That is the magic of those chemicals.

At any rate, even with all my problems, I am still alive.

Despite my difficulties, I kept going to college, but just before my third year I withdrew voluntarily. The medicine had helped widen my range of movement, but I knew it was just a palliative measure. People soon build up resistance to drugs, and the drugs become less effective. Then they have to switch to other drugs, but I put a stop to that process. Ingesting chemicals from outside my body was putting great stress on the organs that break them down, absorb them, and filter them. Apparently my organs were not of the highest quality to begin with, and so they made a lot of noise.

Summer came quickly.

At that time, I was riding around on a 125cc motor scooter. When I was seventeen I got a license to operate medium-sized motorcycles. We had made a date to meet in front of the train station in your town.

At that time, I was torn between a feeling that I had to put some distance between you and me, and a relentless longing for you. I was hesitant to tell you the truth, and you might have found my behavior bewildering.

You got on the back seat of the scooter and we went to a near-by sports park. It was the first time you had ever ridden on the back of a two-wheeled vehicle, so you held me very tight. By the time we got to the park, my back and your chest were drenched with sweat. We talked some nonsense about your chest, but I don't really remember what I was feeling at the time. I guess it was neither here nor there.

We sat next to one another on the park stadium steps.

Just a year before, on the track in this very stadium, I had set a new record in an event with a long tradition. In the whole country there were not a hundred people who could run faster than I, and my goal was to work that down to ten in less than two years.

Now, walking five minutes winded me.

Fantastic.

I was curt with you. I was not capable of misrepresenting myself to the point of being cold to you. But I could pause before answering you, speak in a lower voice than usual, not look you in the face—that was about as much as I could manage.

Even still, it didn't take long for you to notice something about me had changed. But you weren't the sort of person who could ask why. So before long you too were at a loss for words, and soon we were both hanging our heads.

Distancing myself from you.

If I could do that, I hoped you could also distance yourself from me. I mean, I hoped you could find somebody else besides me to love. That way, you would be able to forget about me before too long.

That would be...good.

I could live my life alone.

Actually, I did not think I could possibly live my life alone. I would live my life quietly, with my father and mother to look after me.

And once in a while I would think of you and wonder what you were up to. And I would stand outside in the garden and look at the tomatoes growing, and watch the years go by.

That's how I thought.

So, on this day, I would have to end it.

I decided to pretend that the time I spent with you was incredibly boring. I let out a big fake sigh, and I tried to catch you noticing me looking at my watch and pretending I didn't want you to notice. Sometimes, when you would try to restart the conversation, I pretended to be having trouble feigning interest.

"In my dorm...there's this really strange girl."

"So?"

"Yeah." And you would fumble for words.

"What about her?"

"She...says she wants to be an astronaut."

"Huh?"

"So I was thinking..." And you would fumble for words again. "Every night, she spends a whole hour just brushing her teeth."

"Why's that?"

"She says you can't be an astronaut if you have cavities."

"Wow."

That is what it was like.

And after that, silence. And sighing. And my watch.

I hated that guy.

This was repeated a few times, and then you shut up completely. For a long time we didn't say anything and just sat on the concrete steps.

We were in the shadow cast by the stadium itself. Little kids were riding bikes around the outside of the stadium.

I could tell you were holding back tears. Head down, pressing tight the lips through which your eyeteeth poked, you were holding back.

I sighed again. Even I didn't think I could take it this far. But I did.

"Shall we go back?" I asked.

Still with your head down, you nodded.

Not even one hour had passed. I put you on the back of the scooter, same as when we had come here, and we headed back to the station.

You didn't say a thing.

When we got to the station, I asked you, "Should I see you all the way home?"

"It's okay," you said. "It's not far."

"That's right."

If I had not done another thing and just left, it would have been perfect. But I couldn't leave. I really wanted you. I really wanted to be with you. Even trying to be curt and unlikable, what I really wanted was for your feelings to never change, and for you to be with me.

I was a walking oxymoron. These contradictory thoughts were pulling me in two directions. I liked you, so I was trying to push you away, so I wanted you.

We stood there, silent and motionless, side by side on the walkway in front of the station.

"When can I see you again?" you asked, and you must have been very nervous.

"I don't know," I answered. "I'm pretty busy. This and that."

"Really?"

"Yeah." I looked away from you, up at the summer sky, which was bluer than ever.

"I'll write you a letter," you said, summoning all the courage you could muster.

Letters had been the center of our world. If we could erase all that we had been through, the chemistry between us would come undone, and you would lose both your foothold and your protector.

It was up to me to erase it. I was not the right person to be sitting beside you. Next to you should be someone other than me, someone kind and strong.

But...

"I'll be waiting," I said. "Waiting."

What else could I have said?

"I didn't get it at all, did I?"

I still had my arm around Mio's shoulders, and she was still shivering.

"I never even noticed."

"That was what I was hoping for."

"You should have told me. I would have…"

I cut her off. "You were a very serious person. You had a sense of responsibility. You were the sort of person who could make a commitment to spend your life with someone."

"That's…"

"I know. Not just that. I know that even if I had explained to you all the problems I have, you still would have liked me and stayed with me."

"I would have always loved you."

"Yeah. But at that time I thought it wouldn't be right to make you put up with a loser like me. Even if you loved me, you would not have been happy."

"That's not so. If we loved each other so much, and that would go on forever, how could we be unhappy?"

"You're right. But I wasn't capable of thinking that way. I thought happiness came in the form of something you could see with your eyes."

"That's…sad," Mio said. "Happiness is not something you can count, or weigh."

"You're right." By now, even I could see that.

Now, after having shared my life with you for six years. Now that those days were lost.

"I thought I would be able to get out of your life without saying a word. Without making a fuss. Quietly, softly. Like a puddle in the sunshine. Silently disappearing. That was my intention."

We kept on writing letters to each other.

You wrote of a life where nothing had changed, a landscape of routine, free of concerns, and I wrote back. Each time I delayed my reply a little more. At first I waited a week, then ten days, then two weeks.

A little at a time, disappearing.

As Yuji would say, "*Poco poco.*"

When winter arrived, you came home, but I gave some excuse to avoid meeting you. Actually, though, every day at about lunchtime I was lying in bed thinking about nothing but you. I read your letters over and over, and in your handwriting I could see your face.

Around this time I was in a very bad way. I had been to many hospitals, but I had not been able to find a doctor who thought he could return me to my previous state of health.

At first, some part of me still had hope. I could see no reason for this state of affairs to go on forever. That was what I thought.

Over time, though, that hope also faded. What moved in and cozied up was despair.

Someone once said, didn't they, that despair never gets off to a good start.

Looking back now I think that, more than my troubles themselves, the thing that troubled me the most was the prospect that I would have these troubles my whole life.

I wanted to see you again.

I wanted to be beside you.

But I stifled these desires.

And just like that another half-year went by.

You finished up at junior college, and as I said before you started working as a dance instructor at a fitness club. I dropped out of college and got a job at a convenience store in my neighborhood. I continued my stubborn efforts to expand the radius of the circle that defined my world.

It was also around this time that the content of your letters started to change. Of course this was only natural since you were no longer a student, and were now a full-fledged member of society, but it made me feel a bit lonely to think you were changing into a person I no longer knew.

Only you were looking forward, moving ahead.

I had not advanced a single step since the spring of my nineteenth year.

Before, the view of your back had always been visible, just an arm's length in front of me, but now you were far ahead.

You seemed to be having fun. Several names I didn't recognize started to appear in your letters. Reading the episodes you wrote about unself-consciously, it was easy for me to imagine, "Oh, that guy must like her."

You were pulling away from me, and closer to someone else, a little at a time.

*Poco poco.*

I told myself this was fine.

This was exactly what I had wanted, wasn't it?

That's right, I answered myself.

And then one day I wrote you a letter.

*Due to unforeseeable circumstances I may never be able to write to you again.*

*Please forgive me.*

*Goodbye.*

Lots of letters from you continued to arrive after that.

You never asked what the "unforeseeable circumstances" were. You continued to write about the things that were going on around you, but in words that were perhaps toned down a little, at intervals that were perhaps lengthened out a little.

Then, on the Thursday of the third week in August, you unexpectedly turned up at the store where I worked.

"How are you?" you asked.

"I'm fine."

"You lost weight."

"Hmm. Maybe so."

You had become a very beautiful woman. Your hair had grown long. You were wearing makeup and fashionable clothes. You looked like a chic grown-up.

I couldn't understand anything anymore. I wanted to cry from sheer nostalgia and sentimentality. Confusion and anxiety added to my impulse to cry.

But you started crying first.

All of a sudden.

"Forgive me," you said. Then you wiped your tears with your index finger, rolled your eyes, and laughed.

"I wonder why? Because I hadn't seen you in such a long time?"

"I think so."

That was all I could say.

"Wasn't it a problem for you, that I just showed up like that?"

I shook my head back and forth.

"I'm so sorry," you said again. "I can't go on like this..."

"How's working at the fitness club? Is it fun?"

I tried desperately to change the subject.

"Sure. It's fun in a different way than rhythmic gymnastics."

"That's good."

"Aio, what happened to you and college?"

I was sure you had gone to my house and talked to my mother, who told you where to find me, but you still may have found it strange that I was working in the middle of the afternoon. Classes or no classes, I had always gone to the campus every morning for track practice.

"I quit," I answered flatly.

"Why?" you asked with a puzzled expression.

"I had a lot of things I had to take care of," I lied.

"You mean, like working here?"

"No, not that." I had finally started to relax a bit, and began playing my other self again. "I have a lot of plans. A lot."

"A lot?"

"Yeah."

"I didn't know," you said, your face desolate.

I had no plans. Growing tomatoes is hardly a plan. But I still could not bring myself to tell you the truth.

"I may be leaving this town," I lied.

"Will you be going far?"

"Maybe."

"Overseas?"

I shrugged my shoulders as if to say, "Who knows?"

"And your letters, is that why...?"

I nodded my head lightly about three times, in an incredibly cheesy way. My act was so stiff, you couldn't have helped but notice how unnatural it was if you had been your normal self.

"I'm sorry," I said. My words seemed very cold, even to me. "I don't love you, but I feel some responsibility. And so I'm sorry."

"But I did read your letters, Enokida. Thank you very much."

"Sure."

You seemed to regret having come to the store. But you decided to summon your courage, and you looked up.

"We..." you said. "What now? Sometime..."

You could barely get the words out, and you looked at me with sad eyes.

"It will be nice if we meet again someday. At reunions, or at our weddings."

I can still see your eyes at that moment. You wanted something very badly, and your gaze was stern. What you wanted was the truth. Not the words you had just heard, but the real truth.

I ignored your unspoken plea.

"I want you to be happy. You have done a lot for me."

"My…" was all you could say. You closed your mouth and looked at your feet.

Much later, I asked you what you had been trying to say.

This is what you told me.

"My happiness would be to marry you."

But there was simply no way you could have said that.

"Goodbye," I said. "I have to get back to work."

"Yeah."

"Take care of yourself."

"Yeah."

I left you there and went back into the store.

"That was just fine," I mumbled.

"Really?" I felt someone respond.

And at that, we should have gone our separate ways and lived our separate lives, never to meet again. Our relationship had been reset. All you had to do was follow a life path that would be right for you. For me, a half-assed life lay ahead. I was sure of that.

It may have been a good time to break up. You would be able to find a new love without being dragged down by your past love. No need for hindsight, or to feel inferior.

"I'm sorry. This isn't the first time I've held hands with a man."

You would never say anything like that. And I would have a few memories left to savor.

An apricot-colored dress. Long hair bound in a barrette. A mohair sweater. Fingers meeting fingers in my pocket.

And a knitted headband.

Fantastic.

Who could ever need more than this?

Life is over before you know it, so there is no need for a whole pile of memories to relive.

Just one love. Just one lover. Memories from three dates.

That was plenty.

Want too much and you'll get what's coming to you. That was the golden rule of many an old tale.

People who can never get enough never seem to tire of hearing it.

It's the most comforting thing they can think of.

The days that followed were pretty similar to the days that had gone before.

The only thing that changed was that no letters came from you anymore. It was what I had wanted, but when the reality set in, that there would be no letters from you anymore, my feelings of hope for tomorrow were cut in half.

The thing that had made me sure tomorrow would be better than today was that it would bring me one day closer to your next letter. That had been my life for a long while, and now I had a keen sense of loss.

But the days still went by.

Tomorrow was always very similar to today, but every day I did what I had to do. I got on my scooter and went to some hospital, and then spent the rest of the day scanning bar codes at my convenience store. Before long I got good at scouting out the kinds of hospitals that were right for me. The doctors stopped tilting their heads, and the medicines were able to restore me to some semblance of my former self, if only for a while.

And in this way, a whole year passed in a flash.

Wow.

"And then we met again?"

"That's right."

"And what had my life been like? Had I given you up completely?"

"I don't really know," I said. "You never really talked about yourself very much, and I never dared to ask."

"Was that all right?"

"It was okay. I could well imagine you had been through some tough times, and I knew it was a decision you had reached after a lot of thinking."

"But I'm glad," she said. "So, it was because I made some decision that we've had the life we've had?"

"That's right."

In the most intimate gesture she had made so far, Mio pressed her small head against my chest. That gesture seemed to condense many words into one. Of course they were all words about love.

"And then..." she said.

So I went on.


I don't know whether the medicine I was taking at that time was particularly effective, or whether my counseling sessions were starting to do some good, or whether the Eastern medicine approach I had started sometime before was working, but in the summer when I was twenty-one by some miracle I became virtually indistinguishable from my former self.

Most likely it was some temporary recovery, and I was sure it wouldn't last long. It was like exercise hour for a prisoner who was destined to return to his tiny cell.

If that were the case, I resolved to do as much as possible in the time allowed to me, and I went on a seaside trip on my motor scooter. I wanted to see as many new places as possible before being confined again in my own little world. This is true of anything, but if you know you're about to lose something, only then do you know what it is you really want.

I was sure I was satisfied living in my one hundred-miles-in-diameter world.

Of course, I had not completely returned to my former self. In my memory of the worst time, I had anxiety about premonitions, and that was an awful problem. I was hunched over and used handrails, but step by step I emerged from my room and wandered to far-off places.

About halfway through the entire trip, I turned my course inland. I wanted to make a figure eight rather than a circle.

And on that day, for the first time in a year, I heard your voice.

I had been calling home every day. After all, I had set out on this trip despite the precarious state of my health, and my parents were quite worried about me. This was before cell phones were commonplace, so every day I would call home from some public phone to reassure them that everything was okay.

On this particular day, my mom answered, and she told me about your message.

"There is something I want to talk to you about. Please call," you said. "I will wait for you forever."

"You shouldn't make a girl wait." That was not part of the original message—it was my mother herself saying that.

Got it.


What could have happened?

I thought about a variety of possibilities.

Maybe something bad had happened to you. My head filled with images like that. I was the sort of person who worried more than necessary, so it was hard for me to think of any positive possibilities. Maybe you were sick, maybe someone had taken advantage of you, maybe the heel of your shoe had broken—there were any number of possibilities.

If, in such circumstances, what you needed was encouragement from a boyfriend you had broken up with a year before, I had no intention of begrudging you my heart. I wanted to give you comfort and I was willing to give you encouragement. If you had no better friend to turn to than this miserable heart of mine, I thought that fact alone spoke volumes about the straits you must be in, and that made me very anxious for you. I dug all the coins out of my pocket and stacked them on top of the phone.

Carefully I pushed the buttons that would connect me to your home phone number. This wasn't a collect call—I would pay. Even I had that much self-respect.

You answered on the first ring.

I was not expecting you to answer so quickly, and I was rather surprised.

"Aio?" you asked, before I could even get any words out.

"Yeah. It's me."

"Ah, it's your voice."

Hearing your voice again for the first time in a year filled my heart with warmth.

"Were you waiting by the phone? You answered right away."

"Yeah. I was sure you would call."

"Really?"

"Yeah."

I could hear your whispering voice right at my ear.

"What's up?" I asked. "It seemed like you needed to talk to me right away."

"Aio?"

"What is it?"

"Where are you right now?"

"I'm on the road—about 186 miles away from you."

"Yeah?"

"Yeah."

"Can I come to see you?"
Dead air.
"Hello?"
"Yeah."
"Where did you go?"
"I'm right here. I'm in a phone booth, gripping the phone."
"So, answer me."
"Yeah. I was surprised."
"You were surprised, and then..."
"I was happy. Very. But..."
"It's okay."
"What do you mean, 'it's okay'?"
"Don't worry. It'll be fine."
"It'll be fine?"
"Yeah."

And so, for some reason I may never understand, I allowed myself to be overcome by your confidence, and we made a date to meet two days later in some random town.

Only later did I realize that that particular day was the busiest day of the year in that particular town, elevation 2,000 feet. A half-million people were planning to gather there to watch a fireworks display over the lake. A half-million people is far more than the entire population of some countries like Monaco or Lichtenstein. This was a big deal.

You arrived, unaware of any of this. I wondered if we would actually be able to find each other. No matter, the only thing I could do was to have faith in you, and wait.

I ran around all over town looking for another helmet so that you would be able to ride on the backseat. My plan was to give you the red, open-faced helmet I was now wearing, and find another helmet for myself.

I didn't have enough money to buy one, so I hoped to borrow one from a bike shop. After a long search, the one I was able to locate and borrow was an incredibly old, half-cap helmet. Like the kind an older woman would wear to go shopping. It must have been the tackiest-looking helmet ever. Considering that this would be the first time we were seeing each other in a year, I didn't look so hot, but I couldn't let you wear this helmet.

The appointed time was drawing near, so I steered my scooter toward the roundabout where we agreed to meet. It was still a long while before sunset, but people were already arriving and the traffic was terrible.

By the time I finally got there, it was ten minutes past your train's scheduled arrival. The area in front of the station was alive with tourists.

I looked for you in the crowd. There were many women about your age, but I didn't see you. I looked at my watch. It was fifteen minutes past the time we had arranged.

Maybe you weren't there.

No, that couldn't be.

As the tension of my pent-up feelings relaxed, I dropped to the ground.

What had I expected? Meeting you again here in this place, what had I thought would follow? Nothing had changed since a year before.

Still wearing the grimy helmet, I lowered my head. People passed in front of me and behind me. The voices of the crowd, all together, sounded to me as if they told of a single meaning: A-A-A-FINE-EVENING-LIES-AHEAD!!

Everyone was very excited and looking forward to a fine evening.

Even me. Until five minutes ago.

"Aio?"

Looking up, in the midst of the crowd I saw you, your face

covered with tears.

"That helmet," you said, with a smile of relief. "I don't know how I recognized you."

"You're right," I said. "Well then. Let's go. A fine evening awaits us."

At dusk, we were on the shore of the lake.

I did not ask you why you were there, and you made no effort to ask about my feelings. I was happy to see you, but I was still confused. Whether this was something special, just for this day, or whether it was the beginning of a new series of days, I didn't know myself.

You seemed to be very relaxed. Your face suggested that somewhere deep inside you had found an answer, and you had nothing more to worry about. The fact that you had come here was probably your answer.

We sat down on the curbstones that rimmed the lakeside road, our backs to a metal fence, and a broad field of grass in front of us. It was summer, but the breeze was a bit cold—perhaps because of the 2,000-foot elevation.

In the sky, the giant curtain of darkness prepared just for this night was already descending. The people walking in the light of the streetlamps all had happy faces.

The fine evening was beginning.

"Aren't you cold?"

"I'm fine."

But the breeze that came across the lake made you shiver a bit.

I put my arm around your shoulders.

"Thank you," you said. "You're warm."

Finally the first blast of fireworks went off. We could hear the sound echoing off the surrounding mountains and felt it come back to us in an unexpected wave.

"Fantastic," you said.

Yeah.

Once the opening rounds were over, the fireworks really got going, one after the next, soaring skyward. The entire lake was caught up in the wild enthusiasm of a midsummer night. Anybody would have felt the blood rushing to their head and started yelling something.

"Shall we walk?"

"Yeah."

We stood up and headed for the lakeshore. The edge of the lake was crammed with rows and rows of people. From outside this circle, we looked out at the lake.

"I'm glad I came," you said.

"Are you?"

"Yeah. Getting to spend such a long time with you like this…" you said, entwining your arm with mine. Your arm felt thin and cold.

"I will always be beside you," you said, standing beside me, looking out at the lake.

"But…"

"It will be fine. I'm sure."

I abandoned any idea of asking more. The light from the fireworks dyed your face strange colors. I felt the warmth return to your arm, still entwined with mine. We didn't say anything else.

I stopped thinking. I surrendered myself to the happiness you had given me.

Happiness is being next to you.

Finally, the end was nearing.

Just before the last fireworks, there was a short silence. A half-million people, all as one, held their breath. It almost seemed as if you would be able to hear someone swallow.

Gulp.

And then, over the lake, the final fireworks burst in a gigantic, ballooning dome of light.

A few seconds later, the blast reached us. A heavy, sunken, hot blast of wind.

You kept your serious gaze on the lake. Then you noticed the line of my sight, and you looked toward me and smiled.

"That was really scary."

"Sure was."

"I will never forget this night," you said quietly.

We left the lake and tried to get out of town. In front of the old-fashioned houses, lanterns for the end of the O-Bon festival gave off a pale light. We were both still a bit intoxicated from all the light and sound of the fireworks. This feeling of exuberance made us bold.

You said you wouldn't be going home. I did not argue with you. At this point, it was doubtful you would make it home by midnight, even if you got on a train right away. From the time you had decided to come here to meet me, you had never intended to go home.

A lot of other people were not planning to go home either and many of the local facilities had no vacancies. Our intention was to go to another town, over the pass and two towns away, and look for somewhere to spend the night.

The scooter traveled slowly on the dark highway. You still clung to me with all your might. From your shoulder hung a white vinyl bag.

I told you the story of my many problems.

Hearing my story, your face did not show much surprise.

"Somehow I already vaguely understood. There had to be

something like that, or you wouldn't have given up running, right?"

Wow. You're sharp.

"That was also why you tried to push me away from you, isn't it?"

"Maybe so."

"Weren't you lonely?"

"Very."

And then you said, "Me too."

Well before we reached the pass, it started to rain. I figured the weather might take a turn for the worse because there had been no stars in the sky, but still the sudden rain took me by surprise. At first it was just a few drops, but then it came down in buckets. It may have been summer, but we were at 2,000 feet after all. The rain was very cold.

Our bodies chilled quickly. Because I was the sort of person who worries more than necessary, I felt an anxiety attack about to explode. You were extremely cold and if I didn't do something right away, you would get pneumonia.

Just ahead was a pedestrian bridge. There we took shelter from the storm. Even with this protection, the heat was fleeing from our bodies.

Like coins spewing from a slot machine that had hit the jackpot, the rain did not know when to stop.

Stay here or move on—neither seemed to be a good choice. Your lips had lost their color, and they were trembling, and you were hugging yourself tight with both arms. Your wet T-shirt was clinging to you, and I could clearly see the straps of your bra. Your bangs were plastered to your forehead and dripping water down your face.

My anxiety was spreading tangibly through my chest as I looked straight into your eyes. When our eyes met, you smiled at me courageously.

"It'll be fine," you said. "Let's go. Keep going!"

In every person's life there are isolated instances of tremendous importance. For me, this was one of those moments. For you, who would someday become my wife, it must have been the same. Even so, I can hardly remember anything you said then.

Without a bit of hesitation you spoke the words that would decide the course of the rest of your life.

"That was great," you said.

The instant I heard those words, I knew in my heart I wanted to be with you forever.

You were the one who made the decisions about your own life. And you yourself had chosen to walk my path with me. It had been arrogant of me to think that I could deny you that based on some flimsy self-centeredness.

I could not tell what lay ahead of us. Happiness must be rolling around out there somewhere. If the two of us looked for it together, that would be fun.

"I'm fine," you said.

Fine. I was sure everything would be fine.

It seemed to me as if what you were saying was that our future together would be fine.

At any rate, we would keep going together.

It couldn't be all bad.

Even somebody like me might be able to make you happy.

"Sure," I said. "Shall we get going?"

"Yes, let's."

And the two of us set out in the driving rain.

"By the time we finally found a hotel and checked in, we were both as cold as two corpses in the morgue."

"Wasn't it summer?"

"Yes, but the elevation was over 2,000 feet."

"Dripping wet?"

"And on top of that, we hadn't had anything to eat."

"We might really have died."

"Yeah."

"What happened then?"

"What do you mean?"

"What did we do then? Us."

"Lots of things."

"Like what?"

"We took showers, and we ate some sandwiches."

"Oh."

"And we watched TV, the two of us."

"The kind you have to put coins in?"

"Exactly. We watched a cooking show. What was it? Some sort of broccoli dish, I think."

"We both watched that."

"That's right. I like to watch cooking shows. Not that it does me any good."

"Really?"

"Yeah."

"And then?"

"And then you got into bed with me, and we hugged, and kissed."

"Wow!"

"And we had sex too."

"Wow! We really went for it. Great."

"Actually, not that great."

# 14.

*"Yo, Yuji!"*

Right next to my ear, I could hear that overly familiar male voice, and I flew out of bed.

*"Hey there, look! I brought you a present."*

It seems I had overslept. I got out of the futon, rubbed my eyes, and headed for the kitchen. Breakfast was already on the table. Mio was at the sink, washing something.

"Good morning."

"Good morning. Did you sleep well?"

"Like a log."

"That's nice."

"Aargh!" Yuji said. "Fooled again!"

"That's why..." I said at the breakfast table. "While you

were stuck in bed, I took care of the things around the house. I had to."

It was hard, I said.

"Forgetting, not noticing, getting tired, screwing up."

"So that's why the two of you were running around in dirty clothes, living in a messy apartment."

"That's right."

Mio's face showed she still found some part of the story a little fishy, but finally she nodded.

"I get it. In other words, I have to stay healthy all the time or it's a problem for you."

"Right."

"I said that, right?"

"Huh?"

"'It'll be fine.'"

"Uh, yeah, you did."

"Well, then, I'd better shape up."

"How's your headache?"

"I'm fine. It still hurts a little, but it's getting better."

"That's good."

"Thanks."

Later, I said to her, "This evening, how would you like to go shopping together?"

"Together?"

"There's somebody I'd like you to meet."

"Me?"

I nodded. "A friend of ours. He may be able to help get your memory back."

"Sounds fun."

"Sure."

"Nombre-sensei," Yuji said.

"Nombre…"

"Yes, that's the person we're going to meet this evening. His name is Nombre."

"Is he a teacher?"

"A long time ago," I said. "He used to be an elementary school teacher."

"Pooh will be there too."

Mio made a strange face as she looked at me.

"When you meet them maybe you'll remember," I said.

In the evening the three of us set out for the shopping center, where we bought broccoli, bacon, mushrooms, and cream. On the way home, we stopped in Park No. 17.

We could see Nombre and Pooh right away. I asked Mio and Yuji to wait a minute, and went ahead into the park. Nombre noticed me and waved.

"Hello."

"Hey."

"Are you ready for this?"

"I am. I will not be shocked."

"You have to remember, she's lost all her memory."

"Yes, you told me."

"Also, she doesn't realize she's a ghost."

"Of course not."

"So, I haven't told her anything about what happened a year ago. I've pretended that nothing happened, and that she has lived together with us the whole time."

"That's good. The facts are too sad."

"So..."

"I understand. Don't worry."

I nodded and turned, waved my hand and called to them.

"She's coming," I said quietly to Nombre.

"Mmm."

Mio and Yuji, hand in hand, walked toward us. Yuji walked straight to Pooh and started playing around.

"Hello," Mio said.

"Hello. I hear you're having some trouble remembering things."

"That's right. It's a problem."

"Do you know who I am?"

"I'm sorry," Mio said. "I know that your name is Nombre. But I can't say I remember you."

Nombre gave a pleasant smile.

"Well, considering you've forgotten your husband, if you remembered me that would be a problem."

"You have a point."

Watching Mio and Nombre talk gave me a very strange feeling. It reinforced the notion that she was really here, in this world. Until now, I thought only Yuji and I could see her, that she was some kind of dream of happiness. But now it was obvious that was not the case.

She was really here.

Mio and Nombre were talking about the first time they had ever met.

"You wore your hair down. You were wearing an apron, and you had plastic shopping bags in your hands."

"Right here?"

"That's right. The two of you looked like a couple of high school kids. Not to say you don't still look young."

"What can I say, you seemed happy," Nombre said. "Every day must have been so much fun. That's what it seemed like. It was all so far from my own life, I even felt a little envious."

"Well, our dreams had finally come true and we were able to be together."

"That's right, so I heard. The fireworks at the lake. When I met the two of you here, it must have been the spring of the following year."

Mio turned to look at me.

"That's right. We got married just one year after we got back together. It was the spring when we were twenty-two. I had found a job, and we moved to this town."

"You were always looking out for Takkun. Even when we were standing here talking, you always paid attention and asked him if he was okay."

"I did?"

"Yes, you did. He had just started working, and he was not very healthy. He was trying hard, but you could see the strain. It was painful."

Mio looked at me again and shrugged her shoulders.

It wasn't so bad.

"And life went on like that, and you got pregnant. You were very happy when you told me."

"Yuji was in my belly."

"Huh?" Yuji said.

"We're talking about when you were in my belly. Thanks to you, your mom and dad had the happiest faces in the world."

"Really?"

"Really," Mio said.

"Your mom," Nombre began. "Before you were born your mom was sure you were a boy, and she started buying boys' clothes really early."

"That's right. When Yuji was born it was such a relief. I thought, what if I bought all these clothes for nothing?"

"Huh," Yuji said, not very interested.

"And then..." Mio said.

"This is Pooh!"

Pooh had walked to Mio's feet, and said, "~?"

"What's wrong with his bark?" Mio asked, looking at Nombre.

"Before he came to live with me, he had an operation so he

wouldn't bark, and since then he hasn't had any voice at all."

"~?"

"It doesn't seem to bother him. He's a great dog."

"Well then," Nombre said. He picked up his plastic bag and showed us.

"This is…"

"Smelts?"

"That's right. Half-price today. Makes me happy."

"Mio," Nombre said.

"Yes?"

"I look forward to seeing you again."

"Yes."

"You…" he started to say, but then he faltered. His hand, with the plastic bag, trembled slightly. "You are a lot like my sister. I couldn't tell you how exactly, but something in the way you move.

"It reminds me of old times.

"I remember a long time ago—when I would come home from work and tell my sister all about my day." Nombre was nodding to his own speech. "I'm sorry to make you listen to an old man like me. Don't hesitate to come back again."

"Of course I'll come back. I like hearing what you have to say. I want you to tell me more."

Nombre was still nodding. Then he turned his back to us and headed home. Pooh scrambled after him.

"Bye-bye," Yuji said, waving.

# 15.

Little by little, one piece at a time, she was filling in the blanks I had created.

*Poco poco.*

When my eyes opened in the middle of the night, I could hear her sleeping. Like a fisherman hearing the sound of waves, I had become deeply accustomed to the sound of the sleeping breath of the ghost of my wife.

It made me happy.

Our story, which had begun in the spring when we were fifteen, had progressed to the summer of our twenty-third year.

When Yuji was born, your chest got incredibly big. Your

breasts, which were ordinarily on the small side, rose proudly, aiming at heaven. Baby-blue blood vessels spread over them in a beautiful pattern like the veins of a leaf. Your milk was like a spring at the base of a mountain, never running dry. Yuji could fill his belly, and his mother's milk would continue to spew like a volcano, covering his face. You could tell when he was hungry by the swelling of your breasts.

"Soon," you would say. "Soon he will be hungry and he will cry to let me know."

And so it would be.

The two of you were still bound to one another, as one being.

Your health was giving you trouble, and you weren't really yourself, but even so you did everything you could for Yuji. Yuji was still just like some strange, soft, squishy organism, but we both took meticulous care of him.

We would bathe him together, me holding him and you using a piece of gauze to wash him. After you nursed him, I would burp him. When he would cry and couldn't sleep, I would put him on my stomach, and you would sing lullabies beside us.

*"Nen-nen kororiyo. Okororiyo."*

That put him to sleep in an instant.

I would stare with some annoyance at the sleeping Yuji on my stomach. With him there, I wouldn't be able to move for some time. This was when I first realized the deep affinity between myself and father Emperor penguins.

When the weekend came, the three of us went to the forest.

Mio used my bicycle, the one I ride to work. She may have lost her memory, but she hadn't forgotten how to ride a bicycle.

At the entrance to the forest, mother and child looked for four-leaf clovers. I ran the course that circled the park, and each time I passed them they showed me what they had found. There were a lot of them! It may actually be that in this particular field, four-leaf is simply the normal form for clover.

What a happy place this is!

The days passed quietly.

The rainy season showed no sign of ending.

We met Nombre almost every day. Mio always looked happy to hear his stories of when we were first married. And in the evening I took over his role.

Yuji's first words were "Mamma, Mamma." It wasn't obvious to us whether he meant his mother or the milk that came from her breast. The milk and the breast were a harmonious whole—the distinction between them wasn't clear.

"Mamma, Mamma."

When he said this he was demanding his mother, and also demanding the warm fluid that filled his empty stomach.

Yuji never said "Papa." He heard Mio call me "Takkun," and that's what I became in his mind as well. This emaciated, unhealthy-looking man was "Takkun."

"I called you 'Takkun' too?"

"Yes, you did. From the time we were married, that's what you decided to call me."

"Decided?"

"Yeah. We were such a serious couple. We had to make a decision."

"I couldn't just call you Darling?"

"That wasn't it. You called me all kinds of different things depending on how you were feeling. 'Takkun,' 'Darling,' 'Aio-kun.' But we did make a decision about the basic form."

"What do you most like to be called?"

I thought for a while before answering her. "I like whatever you choose to call me. They are all me, after all."

"In that case, you wouldn't mind if I just called you 'Darling'?"

"I wouldn't mind at all. I'm already getting used to it."

"Well then, just until my memory returns, I'll call you Darling."

"Fine."

# 16.

On our second weekend, we went to the forest again.

It had rained half the night, but then it stopped.

The leaves of the trees were wet with droplets, and the ground beneath our feet was soggy.

We walked slowly along the forest paths. Mio and Yuji had gotten off their bicycles and were pushing them along.

After the rain, spiders had spun many webs across the path, and we had to go slow to avoid getting them in our faces.

"Look, here's another one!"

I pulled a spider's web from my head.

"Why are there so many spider's webs after it rains?" asked Mio from behind me.

"I wonder. The spiders might be in a hurry to rebuild webs that have been wrecked by the rain, but I don't know why they seem to spin so many across the path."

"In the end, the webs across the path just get wrecked again as the people pass by."

"Just can't shake that bunch, huh?"

After we had gone along a bit further, I stopped.

"Let me show you something good."

"What is it?"

"What, what?"

"I did show you the same thing before, at about this time of year. I bet Yuji remembers."

"Really?"

I left the path and headed deeper into the woods. Yuji and Mio left their bikes and followed me. It was hard to walk, because the undergrowth was thick, and there were layers and layers of fluffy fallen leaves. After going about 150 feet, I stopped again.

"Look!"

I moved to the side so I wouldn't be blocking their view.

"Wow! Flowers!" Yuji yelled. "Lots!"

They were hostas. All around, the whole forest floor was covered with the white flowers of hundreds and hundreds of hostas.

"You don't remember? I showed you this before."

"When?"

"The year before last."

One year before we had been busy with Mio, and we didn't come to the forest for a while.

"The year before last? How long ago was that? Was I born yet?"

"You were born, or I couldn't have brought you here. You were four years old."

"You liar!"

"No, it's the truth."

"That's strange," Yuji seemed to be saying as he tilted his head.

"I don't remember at all."

That's my son. Great memory.

"But, they're really pretty!"

He looked at the flowers with a strangely mature gaze.

"I've really gotten something out of coming here."

"What do you mean?"

"Well," Yuji said, looking up at me. "Isn't it because I forgot I saw this before that it seems so great to me now?"

"Ah, well, that may be so."

"Isn't it always? The first time you do something, you get all nervous."

"That's true."

Here and there around the hostas were mountain lilies.

"They smell sweet," Mio said. "I feel like I'm going to smother."

"Why are they so fragrant I wonder?"

"Aren't they just like we were in high school?"

"What do you mean?"

*"Is anybody there? Looking for a partner in love."*

"I see what you mean."

If the flowers were trying to attract insects in order to be pollinated, that too might be seen as a kind of euphemistic love call.

We emerged from the woods.

Beneath the thin clouds covering the sky, the factory ruins spread before us. Door No. 5 looked small.

"Somehow..." Mio said. "Somehow I feel like my whole life began right here."

Yuji parked his bicycle and scampered off.

"Could it really have been just half a month ago?"

"Yeah."

"Your life has been going on since long before that. You lived with Yuji and me."

"Yeah. Knowing that has made me very happy."

Mio stretched her arms above her head.

"But…" she began. "I feel like I've really gotten something out of coming here."

"Really?"

"Sure. I've been able to fall in love with you all over again," Mio said, putting both hands to her chest. "Pitter-pat."


Pitter-pat.


The sound of a heart clamoring.

We held hands as we started walking again.

"Takkuuun!" Yuji yelled. "Look! There's a spring!"

I waved my hand to him in reply.

"A coil spring," I explained to Mio. "Not a big deal. With a little luck anyone can find one."

"Really?"

"Yeah. Sprockets, though, are rare, and finding one is a big deal. Anybody who finds one is really lucky."

"Maybe I should look for one then."

"Go ahead. It's not that easy."

"We found lots of four-leaf clovers, didn't we?"

"That's because there was something special about that place."

"I wonder. Maybe it's just because I am a really lucky person."

"You're right."

"Yuji, I'm coming to look with you," she said, and ran to

catch up with him. Her flowered, flared skirt danced up around her as she ran. Yuji waved to her.

A scene of pure happiness.

If that is what she thinks, it must be so.

And if that is the case, I want her to be happy until the very end. I have never been blessed with much luck myself, but Mio was a woman well suited to the smile of happiness.

From the veranda of our apartment on the second floor, we had a clear view of the vacant lot across the street, right below us. Yuji lost no time burying the day's spoils there. Fifteen bolts, twelve nuts, three coil springs. No sprockets.

Yuji's golden hair sparkled in the sunlight that pierced through the clouds.

"He has beautiful hair," said Mio, standing beside me.

"Yes he does. That's because he's an English prince."

"English prince?"

"That's right. If he just stands there with his mouth shut, anyone might take him for the scion of some noble family. Like an English prince."

"'If he keeps his mouth shut?'"

"That's right. As long as he keeps his mouth shut."

Mio smiled, as if at some private joke.

"Do you realize…?" she started to ask.

"What?"

"Do you realize he talks just like you?"

I thought for a minute before answering her. "Really?"

"He is really handsome."

"He sure is. He looks just like me."

Mio glanced at me, and then returned her gaze to Yuji in the vacant lot.

"Kind. Calm. Straightforward."

"A little bit different from most kids," I said.

"I think that's just part of his charm. That individuality is something very important."

"I wonder."

"I'm sure. Yuji is my one great masterpiece," she said. "To think that such a magnificent child could have come from ordinary old me. It's amazing."

"He is your child, no question about it. Half of his amazingness he got from you."

"Incredible."

"But true," I said. "You forget."

"Do I?"

"Yeah. You yourself were really something."

"Really something?"

"Yeah. Really something."

"Did he get that hair color from your side?"

Mio squinted and looked hard at Yuji. In the end, she didn't wear the eyeglasses. She tried them, but said the prescription wasn't right.

"Yeah, when I was a kid my hair was that color."

"It's a pretty color."

"Mmm. When I was two or three years old, my hair was an even lighter gold. And in the winter my cheeks would be bright red."

"You must have been really cute."

"Who was cute?" asked Yuji, looking up at us from below.

"Somebody whose nose is always runny, who likes to collect useless garbage, and who has a habit of saying 'Really?' all the time."

"Who could that be? Somebody pretty strange..."

# 17.

It was a new month, and the rainy season was about half over.

For the past several days, Nombre had not appeared in the park. I said he probably had other things to do, but Mio just shook her head weakly, with a sunken face.

Four, then five days passed, and still no Nombre. No Pooh either.

"Something must have happened to him," I said.

"Yeah. Should we go to his house? What do you think?"

But actually, we didn't know where he lived. We didn't even know his real name.

"How old is he?"

"I wonder. About the same age as my boss, I think."

"So, how old is your boss?"

"I'm not sure. Let me think."

I was sure it had been a long time since he turned eighty.

"He might have gotten sick."

"Could be."

"We should ask somebody in the park."

"Let's."

There was one young man who was usually in Park No. 17, always reading the same book.

One day, I wondered what it was he was reading, and I snuck up close enough to read the cover. It was *The Dictionary of Useful Things for Everyday Living*.

The young man noticed me. "Everything important," he said, showing me the book, "is written in here."

"Yeah. That's right."

I even asked him about himself once.

"I'm a writer," he said proudly. "But I haven't yet published a single book."

Is that a fact?

If anybody could claim to be a writer without publishing a single book, then everybody in the whole world could claim to be a writer.

So I said to him, "I'm a writer too. But I haven't yet published a single book either."

"I thought so," the young man said. "I could smell it."

"What are you writing?" he asked me, so I said, "I haven't written anything yet."

That was, of course, before I started writing this book.

"I will write something someday though. About my memories of my wife."

"That's good," he said. "People who at least know what they

want to write must be happy."

"Really?"

"Take me for instance. Every time I get a flash of inspiration about what I might like to write, I find out it's already in this book," he said, holding up *The Dictionary of Useful Things for Everyday Living* for me to see. I felt really sorry for him.

Once again, on this particular day, he was in Park No. 17. As always, he was sitting on the bench farthest from the entrance, reading the same book as always.

I told Mio and Yuji to stay where they were while I walked over to talk to the young man. He noticed me as I approached and looked up from his book.

"Hello," I said.

"Oh, it's you is it?"

"That's right. It's me."

He quickly lost interest and turned back to his book.

I got a little nervous as I said to him, "That…"

He lifted his head again. "What is it?"

"You know the old man who always sits on that bench?" As I said this, I pointed to the bench where Nombre always sat. The young man nodded in a relaxed way.

"Sure, I know him. Mr. Toyama."

"Toyama? Is that Nombre's real name?"

"Nombre?" He searched his memory for three seconds. "Ah!" he said. "Nombre-sensei. That's right. I've heard that before. That's right, Mr. Toyama."

"He hasn't been here for a few days."

"I heard he's home in bed."

"No!"

"Really."

"How is he?"

"It's not life-threatening. I forget if somebody said it was his brain, or his circulatory system…"

He closed the book in his hand with a snap. He seemed to be more interested in talking to me.

"But there were complications. He'll never be the same."

I looked back at Mio. Seeing the look on my face, she ran over to me. My expression must have been very grave. Yuji followed behind her.

"How is he?" she asked.

I told her exactly what the young man had told me.

"Oh, my…"

He went on, "They decided he should go to some facility in a town far away. He was going to be taken there straight from the hospital."

"Who took care of all the paperwork and everything?"

"The head of the town board. He's always sticking his nose into everything. He likes doing that kind of stuff."

"How come you know all this?"

"I'm his son. The head of the town board is my father."

"I see."

I asked for Nombre's address, and we left the park.

"What about Pooh?" Yuji asked.

"He'll be okay," Mio said. "He'll be okay."


"There was so much more I wanted to talk to him about," I said on the way home. "Lots more."

"Yeah," said Mio, kicking a pebble at the edge of the road.


"You need him, don't you."

"Mio, you need him too."

"Yeah. You're right." She nodded a little. "I do."

"But…" she said, looking up. "It's not that we can't see him again."

"What do you mean?"

"We can go visit him."

"I don't think that's possible. He's in a town far away."

"It'll be okay," Mio said. "It'll be okay."

# 18.

The next day, in the evening, we went to Nombre's home address, which the young man had given us. The house was about a ten minute walk north of Park No. 17, in an old residential area.

The house was a very old, one-story wooden building. This kind of very simple house used to be called a "modern residence."

The house was surrounded by all kinds of trees and bushes: lilacs, hydrangeas, cotton roses, kumquats. To the right was a vacant lot, and to the left an old apartment building.

Opening the wooden gate, we entered the garden. Stepping stones led to the sliding door of the house. Yuji, who was leading the way, yelled, "Look, Pooh's here!"

Pooh had burrowed under the edge of the house and just his head was poking out.

"Pooh!" Yuji shouted, and the dog looked up.

"~?" His whisper was fainter than ever. Pooh stuck out his tongue, breathing rapidly, then shallowly, repeatedly. "Hah. Hah. Hah. Hah. Hah."

Yuji wrapped his arm around the dog's neck and buried his cheeks in his fur.

"~?"

"He hasn't had a thing to eat."

"So it seems."

The head of the town board may have been a meddler in other people's business, but he did not extend the same attention to their dogs.

"At this rate the dog will be headed for the animal shelter."

"No! No way!" Yuji looked up at us and howled plaintively. "No way!"

"I know, I know. So get him out of there."

"Really?"

"Mmm."

We pulled on the line attached to Pooh's collar and dragged him out from under the edge of the house.

"Okay, let's go."

"Give it to me," Yuji said, and I handed him the leash.

"Pooh! Come on!"

No matter how much Yuji pulled, though, Pooh refused to move.

"Pooh, you can't just stay here. Nombre isn't coming back."

"~?"

"Let's go."

"~?"

Yuji looked up at me.

"He doesn't want to leave."

"Mmm."

I squatted down and looked Pooh in the eye.

"I like your attitude," I said to him. "You're a loyal dog and if you keep this up, they'll probably put a bronze statue of you in front of the train station."

"~?"

"But, life is more than just that. Nombre isn't coming back."
Pooh tilted his head.

"That's right. He has to go someplace far away from here."

"~?"

"This is not what Nombre would want you to do. He would want you to live out your own life to the fullest."

His face suggested he was thinking very seriously.

"You are a wise and intelligent dog. So I think you will see my point. Parting is sad, and it is hard. But you can't just keep standing here."

I got up and gave him time to think. Pooh looked up at me and then at Yuji. And then, as if that effort alone had exhausted him, he dropped his jaw, his tongue flopped out, and he closed his eyes.

I looked at Mio. She nodded, as if to say we should wait a little longer. Yuji also stood and stared in silence.

Pooh looked up at me again and for a long time he continued his shallow breathing.

Finally, he got up. He lifted his head and looked at me.

"Have you made up your mind?"

Pooh nodded—or seemed to.

"Yuji."

"Mmm."

Slowly Yuji started walking, pulling on the line. Pooh followed in silence. They walked through the shrubs in the garden. I opened the gate to the street. Yuji and Pooh walked past me to the outside.

"This is goodbye," Yuji said.

"A lot of things happened here. It's sad."

Pooh looked back at the house where he had lived for so many years. And then, without any hurry, he raised his head high and let out a howl.

"Hew-wick?"

All together, we each looked our separate ways. None of us realized this bizarre sound was coming from the scruffy dog at our feet.

"Hew-wick?" Pooh howled again.

"It's Pooh!" Yuji shouted. "Pooh talked!"

"Pooh can talk!"

Hew-wick?

It was the sound of a wind passing through that narrow gap.

"I wonder if he's saying goodbye?"

"I think so."

"It sounds like he's asking something."

"Mmm."

Hew-wick?

That sound may have been Pooh's farewell to his master who had suddenly disappeared. Or he may have been asking the great "Somebody" in the sky to explain his unreasonable fate. The scruffy dog with the missing vocal chords was looking up to heaven and keening repeatedly in a thin, sad voice.

For now, we decided Pooh could spend one night in the entryway of our apartment. We didn't know what he ate, so we gave him rice and potato salad. With no hesitation whatsoever, he dug right in. He must have been really hungry.

"Tomorrow, first thing, we'll have to take him to the animal shelter."

"Can't we keep him?" Yuji asked.

"I'm afraid we can't. That's the rules of the apartment building. No animals."

"Maybe we can find someone else who can keep him?"

Quietly I shook my head.

"Pooh is an old dog. Frankly, he looks pretty bad."

"Maybe we could let him live in a field near here someplace, and we could feed him."

"If we did that he would be sure to find his way back to his old house. At some point he would end up at the animal shelter for sure."

"What kind of place is the animal shelter?"

"It's a privately operated facility. We would donate some money, and they would take care of Pooh. He would have lots of other animal friends there."

In principle, the animal shelter provides temporary care until a permanent home can be found, but in the case of an old dog like Pooh, it was likely to be his last stop.

"Do you think Pooh will be happy there?"

"I think that depends on Pooh."

"So some dogs are unhappy?"

"Same as anyplace."

With a very serious gaze, Yuji stared at Pooh, who continued to eat potato salad.

"We have to get an early start tomorrow," I said.

"Sleep well."

"Hew-wick?"

"Yeah. You too."

After dinner, I checked the phone book for the number of the head of the town board, and called him. We had stopped by earlier when we went to Nombre's house, but no one was home.

Now he was home.

I asked how Nombre was doing, and the chairman told me it was a disease of the blood vessels in the brain. As his son had said, it was not life-threatening, but it seemed there had been complications. His limbs were partly paralyzed, and he was still disoriented. I said I planned to go visit him the next day, because I was off from work, but the chairman discouraged me.

"He can't really converse yet. It would just be hard for him and for you too."

"I heard he is going to be transferred to some other facility."

"Yes, but not right away. He'll be in this hospital for a while."

I asked the location of the hospital, said a polite goodbye, and ended the call.

"How is he?" Mio asked.

"The chairman asked me to put off going to see him."

"Is that so?"

"You'll go with me, won't you?"

"When, do you think?"

"I don't know."

"Right," Mio said. "Sure I will. I want to go with you. I want to see him."

"Mmm. Whenever."

"Yeah. Whenever."

# 19.

When I woke up the next morning Pooh wasn't there.

I quickly realized this was Yuji's doing. His little shoes had been taken out of the shoebox and were lying in the concrete entryway.

He was sleeping, but when I pulled back his blanket I could see that over his pajamas he was wearing a yellow windbreaker. I imagined he had snuck out in the night looking like this.

"Yuji."

The sound of my voice startled him, and he opened his eyes.

"Takkun. Good morning."

I wished him a good morning too, and then I asked him, "Where is Pooh?"

Yuji looked away and made no sign of answering.

"Well?" I said, sitting down by his pillow. "I said yesterday, didn't I, that Pooh has to go someplace he belongs, or he'll end up at the shelter anyway."

"But…"

"I understand you want to be with him, but you have to think about Pooh too."

Yuji looked up and pierced me with an accusing gaze.

"I have thought about him."

"Really?"

"Yeah. I think Pooh would be happier being with me."

"That's true," I said, combing my fingers through his soft hair. "But we would be living on pins and needles, worried all the time."

"Pins and needles?"

"That's right. Eating dinner, taking a nap, we would be on pins and needles all the time. Worried that somebody would come to get him."

"What would they do if they got him?"

"If they got him they would take him to the animal shelter."

"And then?"

"And then they would wait for somebody else to come and take care of him."

"What if nobody came?"

I couldn't answer. I kept silent, looking Yuji in the eye.

"What if nobody came?" he repeated.

I shook my head quietly.

"Well…"

"No good," he said. "No good."

He got up from the futon, pulled my sleeve, and headed for the front door. In the kitchen, Mio was making breakfast.

"We'll be right back," I said to her, and Yuji and I headed outside. As I suspected, Yuji went straight for the vacant lot behind the apartment building.

"Huh?" said Yuji, looking around.

"What's wrong?"

"He was here," he said, pointing to an abandoned scooter. "I tied him with the line, but now he's gone."

There certainly was a line tied to the wheel of the scooter.

"He must have run away."

Having finished making breakfast, Mio joined us as we searched the area, but Pooh was nowhere to be found.

It started to rain, and we got soaking wet, but we did not abandon our search. We checked at Nombre's house, but the dog wasn't there either.

And then it really started to rain.

"What shall we do?"

"Maybe we should give up. If we go on like this, we'll all catch cold."

"You're right. Maybe he'll come back tomorrow."

"He won't come back," Yuji said. "He'll never come back now."

On the way back home, Yuji asked me, "Do you think they'll catch Pooh and take him to the animal shelter?"

"Possibly. Maybe some curious person will just find him and take him home."

"What if they catch him?"

"I'll ask the animal shelter to let us know if somebody brings in a scruffy dog that goes 'Hew-wick?' If they do, then we can go get him. But then we're going to take him back to the animal shelter again."

Yuji smiled, relieved. "Sure. That'll be fine."

"Okay then. It's settled."

## 20.

The next day, I was the only one with a fever. Mio and Yuji looked at me with strange expressions on their faces. As if they were looking at someone who caught cold just from washing his face. It seems my immune system is pretty poor quality. Like the defense network of some country that has suffered deep cuts in its budget and personnel. Easily yielding to any invasion.

On average, I get a cold and fever about ten times a year. Just by chance, one of those times happens to be now. It's not anything rare or strange.

I snuggled up in the futon and ate an apple Mio had peeled for me.

"Wow!" Yuji said. "Cool!"

"If you catch cold she'll do the same for you."

"Really?"

The truth was, though, my virtuous son rarely caught cold. As a single father, I had been very glad of that.

Yuji went to school, though reluctantly.

"Is there anything else you'd like to eat?" Mio asked.

"No. I don't have much appetite."

"Okay then. I'll make some banana juice. You'll be able to drink that, right?"

"Sure," I said.

Mio walked to the kitchen. From my current location, lying on the floor, I had a great view of her well-developed calves. The backs of her knees had a faint pattern of veins, and I could see a little bit of the soft part above that. A heartwarming view.

Fantastic.

After a while, she brought a tray with a dewy glass on it.

"You need fluids," she said.

She held the tip of the straw to my mouth. I extended my head, just like a turtle, and sucked on the straw to drink the liquid mixture of banana, milk, and honey. A feeling of well-being spread throughout my body.

"Is it good?"

"It's good," I said. "And it makes me feel good."

"Really? Even though you have a fever?"

"Yeah. Things like this are good for that. I feel more relaxed than I have for a long time."

"Relax some more. You can take it easy."

"Mmm."

She pulled my hands and feet, one at a time, out from under the blanket, so she could clip my nails.

"You know…" she started to say.

"What is it?"

"You know, you could be a little more careful about trimming your nails."

"You think so?"

"You are an adult, after all."

"I hardly feel like an adult."

"Really?"

"Somehow I feel like you and I are still fifteen, in a classroom napping with our heads on the desks, and dreaming."

"That would be nice."

"I think so."

"If that were the case, would you make me your bride again?"

"Of course," I said. "If you can be happy with someone like me."

"I'm happy," she said, standing up to go into the next room.

After a while, I heard her voice.

"I'll buy some things for you."

"Really?"

"Yeah. We have nothing to make for supper. Stuff like that."

"Mmm."

When she came back to this room, it seemed her eyes were red. It may just have been emotion.

She touched her forehead to mine to check my temperature.

"It's pretty high."

"Same as always. My body overreacts to everything."

"But if you aren't careful, you won't be able to get the best of this."

"I know."

"I'll be back as soon as I can."

"Mmm. I'll be here," I said.

About fifteen minutes after she left to go shopping, my fever spiked higher. I got terrible chills, and I felt just awful all over. I pulled the blanket up to my head, but I couldn't stop shaking.

I tried to simply endure it, and before long equilibrium set in. I took the thermometer from next to my pillow and put it in my mouth. The little electronic beep sounded within a minute. The LCD said 104 degrees.

I was seized with anxiety. I pictured Yuji struck dumb and stupefied by my death.

Hypochondriacal delirium.

Hypochondria is like a dog that just goes around and around in circles in the same spot—in other words worrying about the smell of your own backside for no reason. Horrible fantasies can start running amok in your mind at the slightest provocation.

Fever, and the chemicals that had started to leak from their valves, were causing my delusions to run rampant.

I remembered I had an antipyretic medicine I had received from the clinic on some previous visit. I was making great efforts to wean myself from medicines, so I hadn't used it all, and there was still some left. I decided I would take some myself before I lost control.

I crawled off the futon, heading for the kitchen. I took the pouch of medicine from the dish shelf, removed a tablet, and put it in my mouth. I poured some water in a cup and drank. I got back down on my knees and crawled back to the futon.

Okay, now I'll be fine. That's what I told myself. My fever is going to break. Yuji won't be left alone to fend for himself. I tried to listen to what my body was telling me and waited for the change.

Finally, I heard the sound of the switch: *Click!* Somewhere between my heart and my stomach. I was sure I could hear the sound. Later I learned this was the sound of one of my body's sensors reacting vigorously to an alkaloid in the antipyretic.

And the world turned upside-down.

The valve opened full, and the gauge maxed out. Even at that point, the chemicals continued to gush up from somewhere or other. All the muscles of my body, ignoring the commands of my brain, contracted.

My arms and legs skewed in odd directions. My fingers were clenched so tight they could have bent coins in half. My pupils were turned so far up into my head they were looking at my brain. My heartbeat was performing a *capriccio* by Nicolo Paganini. It was a magnificently polished heartbeat.

Often at times like this, I prepare myself for death.

That's when Mio came back from shopping.

"How's your fever?" she said as she entered the bedroom. There she saw me, puffed up like a blowfish, looking off in some impossible direction.

"Oh my God!"

She rushed to my side and threw her arms around me. With great effort I managed to say: "AM-BU-LANCE!"

She nodded, softly replaced the blanket over me, and ran to the phone to call for help.

"It'll be right here."

"Good," I said.

I tried to look at Mio's face, but somehow I was unable to bring it into my field of view. All I could see was the ceiling and the pale wallpaper.

Mio came back over to me, hugged me again, and stroked my hair with her hand.

"What should I do? How can I help you feel better?"

"I'm fine," I said.

I was having trouble breathing, and my voice was no more than a whisper. With great effort, I managed to raise my right hand, and held it out to her. She wrapped her hand around my trembling fist.

"I'm afraid," I said.

"You'll be fine. You'll be fine. The ambulance will be here any minute."

I nodded.

From all the pain, I closed my eyes. The earth was spinning about twenty times its normal speed. If Mio had not been there to hold on to me, centrifugal force would have flung me from the solar system.

Then a great wave came over me, and I inhaled violently.

"What is it?!" she said, bringing her ear to my mouth. "Can't you breathe? Are you in pain?"

"I'm sorry," I said.

"Why? What are you apologizing for?"

"Because I couldn't keep my promise."

"Promise? What promise?"

"I said, we would take, a trip."

In my confused mental state, I forgot that the Mio who was here with me now was a ghost. She was my wife who had lived with me all along.

"I told you, we could go, see the fireworks again."

For sure. Sometime.

"That's right," she said.

And then, always after that she had a slightly lonesome smile.

She might have known even then that this would remain an unfulfilled dream.

"Yes, you did. Let's go then. We should go, together. Hang in there."

I grew more confused.

Her voice seemed very far away.

"I've caused you nothing but trouble. I'm so sorry. Thank you so much for staying with me all this time."

"It's okay. Don't worry about things like that. Maybe you

should stop trying to talk."

On my forehead, I could hear a tiny knocking sound. It may have been Mio's tears.

She kissed my closed eyelids.

"Breathe slowly. Don't try to fight it."

But I was unable to stop trying to say all the things I needed to say.

"Take good care of Yuji. He's just like me, so he may turn out to be like this. It's a hard life, and so, and so…"

As my confusion grew, my awareness of even a few inches before me became a faint mist.

Where am I now? I no longer knew even that.

I…I…

I said.

"It always made me happy just to be beside you. Thank you."

And then

"Goodbye."

# 21.

In the ambulance on the way to the hospital, my mind suddenly cleared. The chemicals flooding my bloodstream changed into something gentler, something harmless.

I could tell I was in a vehicle, for the first time in ages, but it did not make me uneasy. Ambulances were one category of vehicles in which I could feel at ease.

"It's getting better," I said to Mio, who was still holding my hand.

"Really?"

"Really."

I opened my fist and closed it again.

"Look," I said. "I can move."

In my palm were deep fingernail marks. If Mio hadn't just cut my nails, I might have really injured myself.

She sighed and said, "Thank goodness."

"I'm so sorry," I said. "You must have been so worried."

She nodded slightly and gave a relieved smile.

"Thanks to you, my life will be a little shorter."

Only later did I learn that was her ironic sense of humor.

The doctor listened to my symptoms and tested my blood right away to check for allergies. In the end, there was no problem. He looked at me as if he was seeing someone with Munchausen Syndrome. I am used to this look. There was no question my fever was high, so I received an intravenous injection of Ringer's solution, and then I was sent home.

We had to take a taxi, but it caused me no anxiety. My stock-pile of chemicals may have been depleted.

Back at the apartment, I had to take an ice bath. Doctor's orders.

"Aren't you cold?" Mio asked.

"Not at all," I said. "It feels good. I feel like the Ice Man of the Alps."

"Who's that?"

"A man who slept in a glacier for 5,000 years."

"I bet he saw lots of dreams."

"I bet he did."

Mio got some plain yogurt out of the refrigerator, added some honey, and put it by my pillow.

"Would you like to eat something?"

"Sure. I'll try it."

She picked up some yogurt in a spoon and brought it to my mouth. I tilted my head and put it in my mouth.

The coolness felt good. And the scent of honey wafted to my nostrils.

"Did you ever have a fit like that before?" Mio asked.

"Many times," I told her. "That was my third trip in an ambulance."

"So, the last two times—did I go with you?"

"Yes, you did. Yeah, for sure. The last time, you called the ambulance. Both times it was the middle of the night, I think."

With the spoon still in her hand, she stared out the window for a while. It was difficult to gauge her internal state from her silhouette. From the slight tremble of the tip of the spoon, though, I could sense the turmoil in her heart.

I was sure that, as a pragmatic woman, she would see this pain in a pragmatic way.

In her usual voice, thin and high, with a slight tremble at the end of a word, she said, "I wonder, if I weren't here, who would be able to take you to the hospital?"

I might have missed this. She said it so casually, unthinkingly, as if complaining about how the laundry had dried.

"Huh?" I said.

I felt as if I had heard something important. She looked at me and smiled. It was a very kind smile.

"I'm worried about you."


She scooped up some more yogurt and brought it to my mouth. I took a big mouthful and savored its tartness. And then I asked her, "Did you just say, 'If I weren't here'?"

She tilted her head in a funny way. She opened her eyes wide, as if to say, "What do you mean?"

"Just now. You did, didn't you?"

"I guess I did," she said. "When the rainy season is over."

As I heard her words, it suddenly dawned on me.

"Did you recover your memory?"

But she just shook her head slowly. "My memory is still gone. I wish it were back."

"So…"

"I read the book. Your book. I just happened to come across it," she said.

"I was straightening up the closet, and the shoe box fell out, and the book was in it."

It was my turn to nod.

Everything was hidden in that box. The college notebook in which I was writing my book. Different papers she shouldn't see. Receipts from the hospital, papers from the cemetery, all the written documents concerning her death.

I should have put it somewhere more out of reach. But this tiny apartment has no secure locations.

"How long have you known?" I asked.

"About a week."

"I'm sorry I didn't notice until now."

"It's okay. I thought I could just go on like this, not saying anything. As if I didn't know."

"Mmm."

"But I felt there were some things I had to do right."

"What do you mean by 'right'?"

"Making sure the two of you were able to live okay, and I wanted to make sure to say a proper farewell."

"If I told you that book was all a pack of lies, would you believe me?"

She smiled her lonely smile and shook her head.

"What can I say? It was only after I read the book that things made sense. I finally understood the sense of strangeness I had been feeling."

"'Strangeness'?"

"The feeling that I was not of this world. I felt it the whole time. Once I knew the truth in your book, some part of me felt relieved. 'Ah, I am a person from Archive!'"

And also, she said.

"The two of you acted rather suspiciously. Sometimes you talked about us as if everything had happened in the past."

I hadn't realized. I hadn't realized, but she had. My book ended at the point where she came to this apartment. But that was enough. For the rest, there was that pile of documents.

"So, for my sake you didn't say anything?"

I kept silent.

"Don't make that face," she said. "I'll be fine."

"You always say that," I said.

"Because I'm with you."

It's because I am with you that my heart is at peace.

"I want to be with you always."

"Me too. But, I'm sure..."

"Is it up to you to decide?"

"I don't know. I don't know anything. But I did tell you. In the rainy season I will come back to you."

And, she said.

"I think that when the rainy season is over I will have to go back."

"Stay here always."

"How can I stay?"

She was asking a serious question. She wanted to know the answer more than anyone.

"Tell me?"

I could not answer. I don't think anyone would have been able to answer. Maybe someone knew, but they were keeping their mouth shut.

"There is something I've been thinking about that I haven't been able to say," I said.

"What is it?"

"Don't you think you should see your father and mother?"

"How? Just go say, 'Hi, I'm home'?"

"That wouldn't be right."

"Nombre was okay."

"Well, yeah, but…" It would be better not to see them, she said.

"The fact that I have no memory might cause some pain."

"Really?"

She nodded.

"I can't even recall what my father or mother look like. If I see them, I won't have anything to say to them. It would just be hard."

"I wonder."

"I'm sure. It's okay. The less sadness the better, right?"

"I guess so."

"I'm sure."

Then, as if she had just remembered something, she went to the back room and brought back a cookie tin.

"Oh. That."

"I found this at the same time."

"I forgot about that. That's right, they're in there."

Photos.

"This." She picked up one and held it out for me to look at.

"I look different."

It was a photo from the day we got married. She was wearing her wedding dress, and I was in a tuxedo. She was smiling slightly, but I looked tense, and my face was white as a sheet of paper.

"Pretty."

"Me?"

"Of course you."

"Thank you," she said. "You look like there's something wrong."

"A few seconds after that picture was taken, I fainted. All through the ceremony, you kept asking me, 'Are you all right?'"

"Were you in some sort of pain?"

"No more than usual. But I made it through the ceremony."

"Thank you."

"Not at all."

The second photo was a group shot in front of the church.

"This is your father and mother, and your sister and brother," I said, pointing with my finger.

"They look like nice people."

"They are."

"But the ceremony was very small, wasn't it? Is this everybody?"

"That's right. Everybody. Just our families. This big guy behind is the minister."

"A foreigner."

"Yes. Mr. Burdman. He spoke Japanese very well."

"We said our vows before him?"

"Yes, we did."

"And did we keep our vows?"

"Yes, we did. You mean like, 'to love each other in sickness and in health'?"

"That's right."

"We were always that way."


Next came a bunch of photos of our life as a couple, here in this apartment.

"My belly is big in this one."

"Yuji was in there."

"My face was puffy."

"Yeah, it was about that time when you started to get sick."

"Oh, that's right."


"This is Yuji when he was just born, right?"

"Doesn't his face look weird?"

"No it doesn't. He was cute!"

"This one's a little…"

"Yeah," she said.

"It certainly is a little…"

"After about six months he was changing every day. His hair grew in, and the shape of his eyes got clearer."

"What about this one?"

"Yeah. Starting around then."

"You're right. An English prince."

"Absolutely."

"Look, in this picture his hands are full of bolts."

"Come to think of it, he has always liked doing that. His whole life."

"He hasn't changed a bit, has he?"

"He's the type who grows slowly. Same as me."

"Really?"

"I still have some of my baby teeth."

"My, you are a late bloomer, aren't you."

"Come to think of it, I've never had measles either."

Before long, I got tired and fell asleep.

When I woke up again, she was in the next room.

"Mio?" I called out, afraid.

"Are you awake again?" she asked as she entered the room. "Shall we take your temperature?"

My temperature had gone back down to 100 degrees.

"Ah, that's good. It's gone down."

"Yeah. I'm feeling much better now."

So it seems, she said.

"In the future, if you have another seizure like this, what will you do? I may not be here, you know."

"I'll be fine. These seizures are not a matter of life or death. It hurts like hell, and I always think I'm going to die, but I haven't died yet."

"But what if you're all alone?"

"Yuji will be here," I said. "Today it happened to be daytime, but usually my seizures come at night. So Yuji will be here."

He might look like nothing much, but I can count on him. After I said this, she thought a little, and nodded.

"Okay. Fine."

"And, I'll never take that antipyretic again. That's what caused my seizure this time, so I know not to take it again."

"Adding to the list of things you can't do."

"That's all right. It's important to know what I can't do. It's when I don't know, and do something I shouldn't, that I get into trouble."

"You mean like today?"

"Yeah."

"I'm worried," she said. "I'm very worried about leaving you here."

"You always were like that."

"What do you mean?"

"You always were worried about me, and ignored your own needs."

"That's just the way I am."

"But…"

"What is it?"

"Nothing," I said, shaking my head. "Nothing at all."

After that, I hardly felt feverish anymore. Once the pain was gone, loneliness took its place in my heart.

"Mio," I called out.

She sat beside my pillow, pulling the threads from string beans.

"What is it?"

"Come here," I said. "Here."

She looked at my face, and then at the beans in her hand. Her eyes made me think of that time when we were at the station, and she was blowing on her cold hands to warm them. She hesitated for a few seconds, silently, and then said, "Okay, here I come."

"Wow! Cold!"

"Oh, right," I said, and removed the ice packs from the futon. "That's better."

"You're cold too," she said.

"Just like Ice Man."

"Yeah, that's right."

And I put my hands around her slender waist and pulled her to me. She flinched for a second, as if resisting, but she soon relaxed. And then she tucked her head beneath my chin.

"That's nice," I said.

"Hmm? What?"

"Best position."

"Like this?"

"That's right."

"Just what comes naturally."

"We are a couple, after all."

"You're right," she said, jokingly. She may have been a bit embarrassed.

"We should have done this sooner," she said, kissing my neck.

"A love that lasts just six weeks."

"What shall we do?" I asked.

"This," she said. "Just do this."

"I'm home," Yuji said. "Mom?"

We hardly had time to get untangled before Yuji was there in the bedroom with us. Seeing his parents with their arms around each other and panicking, he said, "Oh, my."

## 22.

Slowly, Mio began her preparations to leave this world again. Everything she did was so that Yuji and I would be able to live a little better. She said she would tell Yuji when the time came, but in the meantime she pretended that she didn't know anything. She read books and did a lot of research about my many problems. And she took a trip, two hours by train, and came back with three little tinted bottles.

"Herbal oils," she said. "Lavender and eucalyptus, and sandalwood."

"And what do I do with those?"

"You just let the aroma drift out into the room."

"That's it?"

She nodded.

"These are just like those chemicals you're always talking about. They enter your body and go right to work. They tell you to relax."

"And what if they don't work?"

"Hmm." She thought for a while, and said, "You should sing."

"Sing?"

"That's right. A song like this."

*One elephant began to play*
*Upon a spider's web one day,*
*He found it such tremendous fun*
*That he called for another elephant to come.*

"Ah," I said. "I know that song. Yuji taught it to me."

"Yuji did?"

"He said he learned it from you."

"Well, I must have taught it to him sometime then."

"How did you know this song?"

"I don't remember," she said. "Now I remember. I said you should sing this song if you're having trouble."

"You must have sung it yourself then."

"Yes. When I was having trouble."

Mio put a drop of lavender essence on a tissue. I took it from her and held it up to my nose.

"What do you think?"

"Yeah, it smells good. I don't think I've ever smelled anything like this before," I said. "But it's really familiar too. What is it?"

"What do you mean?"

"Somehow, when I was little…"

"When you were little?"

"Ah, that's it!" I said, sniffing the tissue again. "When I was little, and I would play the harmonica, there was a smell like this."

"A harmonica? Smelled like that?"

"A harmonica my cousin had given me. A great big one. It was made of metal, and it had two rows of holes, top and bottom. When I put my lips on it, it smelled like that."

She seemed skeptical, but then she put some sandalwood essence on a tissue and handed that to me.

"Oh, I know this one."

"Do you?"

"My grandmother's fan."

"What do you mean?"

"No mistaking it. This is the smell of a fan my grandmother had. It was really special."

She tilted her head for some time, then said "Ah!" and clapped her hands. "Maybe so," she said.

"What do you mean?"

"Lots of folding fans have spines made of sandalwood."

"You're right. That's it."

"Next," she said, trying some eucalyptus.

"This is the smell of menthol. That's the only thing it could be."

She smelled it and nodded.

"That's right. I think so too."

"Because you catch cold easily," she said. "You should put one drop of this eucalyptus in a glass of water and gargle with it. Or you could mix it with some neutral oil and coat your throat with it."

"Got it. I'll do that."

"Since you have trouble taking medicines, you have to be careful about catching cold."

"Mmm."

"Your illness has weakened your immune system."

"Is that so?"

"That's right. So you have to be more careful than ordinary people. And you shouldn't eat instant foods either. You have to cook for yourself."

"Okay."

"And eat your vegetables. Even if Yuji says they taste yucky you have to make him eat them."

"We'll be fine. Leave it to me."

Mio looked at my face for a long time, thinking. But she wasn't seeing me. At least not the me that is here now. She was looking at the me of six months from now, or after that.

She said, "That's right."

"Really?"

"I shouldn't be telling this to you. I should be telling Yuji."

"You mean," I said, "you should depend on Yuji rather than on me?"

"For some things, don't you think?"

She gave a quick nod. "I told you before, didn't I? Half of Yuji came from me. I think that half may be someone we can rely on."

"What about the other half?"

"Hmm. In charge of kindness?"

"Ah. I get it."

And with that, Mio started teaching Yuji about housework. How to handle a knife, how to choose good foods. Also how to do laundry, and how to beat it when you hang it out to dry—lots of things like that.

It was lucky for me that Yuji seemed to have the makings of a great housekeeper.

I was like an alternate, not a regular. An old-timer who sits on the bench, watching the young guys getting tips from the coach on technique and footwork. Gnawing the edge of his towel from envy.

Why is it always him.

Still, it was a great thing to watch. Until now, I had been having him help me around the house, but since he was learning by watching his father who was not terribly skilled, he had a little trouble himself. Now, under the tutelage of a superior instructor, all at once his natural talents revealed themselves.

It was obvious that half of him came from Mio. The half of him that was always dopily saying "Really?" and stuff like that obviously came from me.

Well, no matter.

In the evening, while Yuji was watching cartoons on TV, I practiced calligraphy.

"I used to do this, before, because you told me I should."

"Really?"

"You're trying to say, 'So it seems'?"

"A little."

"I thought so."

She read the book to the end. It made her very happy to know I intended it for Yuji to read.

"The boy is still only six. I'm sure he will forget almost everything about me," she said. "I think it's a good thing you write this all down. How we met, and about us right now."

So I have to be able to write it legibly enough for Yuji to be able to read it. That's the story.

"Were my notes hard to read?"

"Well, yeah. Not like the Rosetta Stone or anything, but pretty hard."

"Is that so."

"When Yuji was still a baby."

"A long time ago. If only you had kept on practicing, imagine how beautiful your writing would be by now."

"I did keep it up, for about three months. But then Yuji started crawling around, and I had to give it up."

"He would make a mess of things?"

"You might say that. At any rate, he was very interested. He
would have this 'What are you doing?' look on his face, and try
to grab the ballpoint pen."

"He was cute."

"That's true, but after about the millionth time it gets old.
Why do babies have to do things over and over and over?"

"Don't you think it might be because they can't remember
what they just did?"

"Maybe so. I used to get so mad, I piled up all the futons, like
trenches and breastworks, but Yuji would just climb right over
them, smiling all the way."

"He had a lot of energy."

"You said it. He used to drink your special milk by the gallon.
He had the power of Roger Bannister at his peak."

"Who's that?"

"Someone I know very well."

"Who is it?"

"But he doesn't know me."

"I thought so."

For the record, Roger Bannister was the first human being to
run a mile in under four minutes. Some magazine included him
in its list of the one hundred most important people of the twentieth century. Yuji is in good company.

# 23.

On the weekend, we went to the botanical gardens.

I brought along an old Minolta camera my grandfather had given me a long time ago.

"I wonder if I'll show up?"

"Don't worry. I'm sure you're really here."

Like old times, we rode on the bicycle with me pedaling and Mio in the back. Yuji, on his kid's bike, brought up the rear.

"You don't ride the scooter anymore?" Mio asked.

"No, I got rid of it a while ago. It scared me. I couldn't ride it."

"I think that was a good decision. Those things are dangerous."

"I was always amazed you would ride it at all. No seat belts."

"And," Mio said, "no air bags."

"Ha ha. That's right."

We hadn't been to the botanical gardens in quite some time. When Mio had been feeling well we used to come here once a month or so.

We parked our bicycles at the entrance and went through the gate. There was a stone pavement about 160 feet wide. On the right was a lawn and a sign.

*Flowers now on view,* it said, and there were about ten little plates hanging below.

Dayflowers, geum, clethra, bellflowers...

"Look, it says *hosta sieboldiana*!" Yuji said happily. His voice carried throughout the empty park.

"This park has a lot of hostas! There are *hosta sieboldiana*, and *hosta montana*, and *hosta undulata*, lots of them!"

"You sure do know your hostas!"

"He learned it all from you."

"Really?"

"Yeah. You used to know the names of about two hundred different kinds of flowers. Maybe more. You really, really liked flowers."

"I vaguely remember that."

"Let's go further in. There's a place here you used to really like a lot. Maybe you'll remember it."

"Yeah. Sure."

We walked slowly through the trees.

"This is a horse chestnut."

For each tree we passed, I pointed and said its name. Of course, I had learned all of these names from Mio.

"This is a *whatchamacallit*," Yuji said, laughing.

"*Whatchamacallit*? That's strange," Mio said.

"Apparently it's really called a Chinese fringe tree."

"And this is a lily tree."

"'Lily tree'?"

"Yes, but it's not a lily. In spring it has blossoms that look just like tulips. We used to come here often when the flowers were in bloom."

"What about me?" Yuji asked.

"You were with us. When you were little we used to push you in the stroller."

"Really?"

"Really."

We followed a counterclockwise course around the park, at the very deepest point of which there was a wisteria arbor. At our feet were white clover and burclover. There we spread a picnic cloth and sat down to eat the bento box that Mio and Yuji had prepared.

"I sliced the wieners," Yuji said.

"You should be proud. That could be a useful skill."

"Don't you think?"

"It's quiet here, isn't it?" Mio said.

"There's not many people here today."

"People are attracted to better known flowers. Hydrangeas, lavender, roses, things like that. There aren't many people who will go out of their way to see dayflowers. That's why it's always quiet here."

"I like this place."

"You always said so. Can't you remember?"

"I'm not sure. Somehow, though, I have this ache deep in my heart. Is this what longing feels like?"

"I think it must be."

We finished our lunch, and Yuji ran to a big pond lined with bricks. In the pond there were water lilies, and rushes, and killifish.

"He looks happy."

"That's his favorite place. He could just sit there staring into the water forever."

"Really?"

"Yeah."

Mio stretched and lay back on the cloth. I lay down beside her.

"This feels good."

"Sure does."

Somewhere in the distance we could hear children laughing. Buzzing horseflies approached, then flew away.

"I could fall asleep."

Looking to the side, my eyes met Mio's, who had been looking hard at me.

"The rainy season will be over soon," she said.

"That's true."

"I don't want to leave you two."

I held her small head.

"Yeah, I know."

"I wish this was a dream."

"You do?"

"When I woke up, I would be in the classroom in high school, and you would be beside me."

"Yeah."

"And I would say to you, 'We are going to get married, and have a son who looks just like an English prince.'"

"Yeah."

"And what would you say, do you think?"

"I look forward to a mutually beneficial relationship," I said. "If you'll have me."

We kissed.

"My first kiss," Mio said.

"That was nice," I said. "Would you like some more?"

We took pictures of the three of us, several of them, placing the camera on a stone water fountain and using the timer. Mio and I stood with Yuji between us. We held hands. Right behind us was a myrtle tree, covered with white blossoms.

At the gardening shop across the street from the botanical gardens, we bought a potted plant. Spring flowers were over, and it was time to look forward to autumn flowers.

"What's that called?" asked Yuji.

"Kaguyahime," Mio said.

"Hmm...a Kaguyahime, huh?"

"That's right. I'm going to ask you to take care of it."

"Me?"

"That's right. You'll have to look after it so that it blooms properly in the fall."

"What kind of flowers will it have?"

"Yellow. They're supposed to smell especially good," I said.

"Okay. I'll do it."

"I hope so."

So we took our Kaguyahime and headed back to the apartment.

# 24.

The remaining days seemed to pass more quickly than we would have liked them to.

Mio taught Yuji a few things about cooking, and in the evenings I continued my calligraphy exercises. On my way home from work I stopped in Park No. 17, though Nombre and Pooh were not there. (Nombre had been taken to the faraway facility while I had been in bed with a fever. We only found out much later.) After dinner we took walks along the canal.

Mio and I kissed several times when Yuji wasn't looking.

The TV weather report said the rainy season would end soon. This morning, before dawn, there was a terrible thunderstorm, but that was the kind of rain that typically heralds the end of the rainy season.

Two more days.

Yuji was intent on his breakfast, not listening to the TV.

I looked at Mio.

She was shaking her head, looking like she was about to cry.

Yuji kept on eating, blissful in his ignorance.

That night, Mio and I had sex.

Once we were sure we heard the husky breathing of Yuji's sleep, Mio came over to my futon.

"The last time it took us six years to get this far."

"And this time six weeks. Terrific!"

These days in this country there are probably plenty of couples who get this far in six days. Under the covers, I removed Mio's cotton pajamas. Her body was stiff and passive.

"You've had practice, I see."

"All thanks to you. We have done this more than a few times."

I took off her panties too, and balled them up with her pajamas and set them on the floor. Nervously, she reached out and tucked the white panties under the pajamas. I could see her small breasts jiggle. Seeing where I was looking, she pulled the blanket up to her shoulders.

"What is it?" she said. "Without my clothes, I feel vulnerable. Helpless."

"Really?"

"Yeah. Take yours off. I don't like being the only one."

"Got it."

I stripped off my pajamas and underwear, rolled them up and tossed them aside.

"There. That better?"

We lay side by side, facing each other, and slowly, quietly, our bodies drew closer.

Mio exhaled. "So this is what it's like."

"That's right. But it's not just this."

"Oh my gosh. I hope I can keep up."

"Don't worry. You used to do just fine."

"Okay then. I'll try."

"Is this something you have to try at?"

"Isn't it?"

"I wonder."

It was not fine at all. She was trying so hard nothing was working.

"It hurts."

"You're kidding."

"No, really."

"But…"

"Are you sure you're in the right place?"

I tried focusing all my attention on a single spot.

"I'm sure."

"Well then, what's up?"

From below, she looked uneasily up at me. Supporting my upper body with both hands, I thought for a while.

"Having once left this planet, and getting ready to come back, I wonder if you were cleared on everything?"

"What do you mean, 'cleared'?"

"Like a game. Maybe your history was reset to zero."

"You think so?"

"So you have no memory and no experience," I said. "I bet only the necessary data was input, and that's what you start out with."

"Are you saying you think I'm a virgin?"

"Apparently so."

She was confused.

It was only natural.

Any mother of a six-year-old child, suddenly told she's actually a virgin, would be confused.

"It's okay," I said. "If you trust me. I have plenty of experience with this."

Hearing me say this her expression relaxed.

"Sure. Sure you do."

She closed her eyes and let all the tension drain from her body. As I sank slowly, she arched her back, exposing her pale neck to me. Her lips parted slightly, and she let out a little sound.

"Please. Gently, softly…"

I don't think I was able to do it as deftly as she might have wanted. I thought the first time we ever had sex, years ago, was better. At that time I didn't have the presence of mind to focus so intently on paying attention to her. Before either of us realized what was happening it was all over. This time, for all our greater experience, we got tripped up paying attention to each other. In the end, it just lengthened the time she was hurting.

As Mio lay there, dazed and defenseless, I stared distractedly at her pale breasts, damp with perspiration, like a pair of newborn kittens.

"You did your best. You were great."

Hearing me say this, she smiled faintly.

"What if I said it was nothing, would that be okay?"

"No, you really tried hard."

"Thanks."

"Not at all."

We lay there naked, staring up at the ceiling bathed in pale orange light.

"Takkun," she said. "I'm happy."

"Really?"

"It's been a great six weeks."

"Yeah."

"We fell in love."

"Yes, we did."

"We held hands, and we kissed."

"And we had sex."

"I even became a mother. That's a lot," she said. "Who could wish for anything more than this?"

"Yeah…"

"I'm glad I got to know the two of you."

"Yeah…"

Softly she placed her hands on her chest.

"This may seem a bit strange," she said, tilting her head to look at me, "but at first I was jealous of your wife."

"But you are my wife."

She shook her head.

"I am myself. A girl who just came into this world six weeks ago."

"Mmm. I get it. That's the way you feel."

"I thought it was great, to be so loved by the two of you, to make those great memories."

"Yeah."

"You two look at me with those doe eyes, and I am not me, I am the woman of your memories."

She continued: "That's why I did everything I could do. I was a good wife to you, so that you would love me."

"Yes, you were. And we fell in love. Just like the first time."

"Really?"

"My heart went pitter-pat. I fell in love all over again."

With the newborn you.

Mio looked at me as if at a blinding light. And she showed me that awkward smile, as if she were about to cry.

"I love you so much I don't know what to do."

I reached out my hand, and pulled her to me. Her sweat was

cold and her body was chilly.

"Me too. I bet we end up falling in love like this over and over again. Every time we meet we'll be attracted to one another all over again."

"Somewhere, someday?"

"That's right, somewhere someday. And when that happens I will want to be right beside you. I like it right here."

"Yeah. Me too," she said. "I like being right beside you."

She tucked her head under my chin.

"Best position, right?"

From somewhere near my collarbone, her voice sounded faint.

"We are a couple, after all," I said.

"Yeah. So we are."

"Soon now," she said. "Soon the day will change."

"Are you sleepy?" I asked.

"No, I'm not," she said.

"Tomorrow is Saturday. I don't have to go to work. We'll be fine."

"Well then. Can we stay just like this a little longer?"

"Fine with me. Let's stay just like this a little longer."

"Thanks."

"Not at all."

# 25.

The next day arrived, with little apparent difference from the day before. But this was the day that had been foretold to us as our day of sadness. As on the same day the year before.

Not all stories are filled with happiness. Some stories are sad. Most sad stories are made up of tales of parting. To this day, I have never heard a story of a meeting that did not also involve a parting.

A misty rain was falling quietly on the earth. The sky was smeared a milky white. A cheap sky, depthless.

We put up an umbrella and headed for the forest on foot. Little puddles were everywhere. Yuji had to step in every one of them.

The old sake brewery at the entrance to the forest was making its knock-knock-whoosh noise, as usual. We walked along the forest paths, covered in layers of damp leaves. The wet leaves of chestnut oaks and snowbells plastered the sky. At the edges of the path were little yellow sorrel flowers. Pine seedlings shooting up from the earth, covered with dew, gave off a pale light.

The leaves of the trees kept most of the rain from falling on us. We closed the umbrella, and Mio and Yuji walked hand in hand.

"I want to see the hostas again," Mio said.

"Just a minute. We'll leave the path right up here."

When we got to the spot, there were no more flowers. But the big, beautiful hosta leaves were quaking as they were struck by the rain.

"The flowers are all gone."

"Yes. So it seems."


We reached the edge of the forest. The road had a slight incline. Just ahead, the forest would come to an end.

Mio slowed her pace and looked hard at Yuji who was walking beside her.

"What is it?" asked Yuji, noticing her gaze.

"Mom..."

"Yeah."

But she couldn't bring herself to say it.

"What is it?"

Yuji looked at his mother with an expression torn between hope and fear.

"Mom..." And then finally she was able to say her next words. "Soon I have to say goodbye."

Yuji's face suddenly lost all expression. His lips parted slightly and trembled. He looked at his mother's face for a very long time.

And then he hung his head, as if trying to follow the falling leaves.

"When is soon?" asked Yuji, keeping his gaze on the wet ground.

Mio shook her head.

"I don't know."

"You decided when to leave, didn't you? You remembered, didn't you?"

"No, your dad told me."

"He promised to keep it a secret," Yuji mumbled, still with his head down.

"I asked him. To tell."

"Really?"

"Yes, I did."

And then the two of them fell silent.

Hand in hand, matching their stride, they walked slowly. They looked as if they might have been the first, or the last, two people in the world. No other people could ever take their place. Mother and child walking along as if they were a single life.

I walked behind them, looking vacantly at their backs. Mio was wearing a white dress with a cherry-blossom-pink cardigan draped over her shoulders. The same as on that first day. Yuji was wearing pedal pushers and a yellow long-sleeve T-shirt. At the end of his thin legs he wore boots the same color as his shirt. The boots had pictures of a scruffy dog that looked just like Pooh. Mio had bought them for him. He walked around in those boots even when the weather was fine.

Yuji finally opened his mouth to say something. "Mom?"

His voice was a lot like Mio's, but about three steps higher.

"Mom, I'm sorry," he said.

Mio stopped in her tracks and stooped over to look Yuji in the eye.

"Why are you apologizing?"

She swept her wet hair out of her face and brought her face close to her innocent young son's.

"You haven't done anything wrong."

Yuji shook his head in silence.

"I did do something wrong."

Although he was nearly whispering, his words rose at the tail end as he spoke. In his voice you could hear his pain, something rising in his throat.

"You're a good boy. Don't say things like that."

Mio stroked Yuji's cheek. His nose grew red. He blinked repeatedly.

"It's my fault, isn't it?"

Mio looked up at me in surprise.

I quickly shook my head, and then slowly nodded.

No, it's not his fault.

You know, don't you? My thoughts are as you read them. He...Yuji is as pure as snow that has not yet fallen to the earth.

She nodded back.

*Yes, I know. My thoughts are the same as yours.*

Looking deep into Yuji's eyes, Mio said, "That is not true." Her face was more serious than I had ever seen it. "It isn't true."

"It is too true. I know."

Yuji used his little fists to wipe the tears that were bursting from him.

"Somebody told me. You died because I was born."

He looked up at Mio. His wet hair was plastered to his reddened forehead. His peach-colored lips were pursed in an "O" as he accused his mother.

"I didn't know the whole time."

He blinked repeatedly.

"I didn't know that. If I had known, I would have behaved better."

I'm sorry.

Yuji sniffled.

"I have wanted to apologize for a long time. I am sorry."

I'm sorry.

"Don't apologize," Mio said. "You haven't done a single thing wrong. You're a good boy. You're the best kid in the world."

Her voice seemed like someone else's, trembling and hoarse.

"But…" Yuji sniffled. "If I hadn't been born, you could have lived with Takkun forever, right?"

"No, that's not true."

That's not true.

Mio combed Yuji's wet hair with her fingers.

"Even if I hadn't had you, things would have turned out the same, I think."

Yuji stopped blinking.

"And on top of that, I can't imagine my life without you. Only by getting to know you have I been able to feel that I have lived my own life. That's what I think."

"Really?"

"Yeah. If I hadn't known you I would never have experienced this feeling of fulfillment, even if I lived fifty years."

"Really?"

"Yeah, really. You are the reason your mom and dad met. So that we could get to know you."

"Me?"

"That's right. You. You who are different than anybody else. My very own English prince."

"Who?"

"Somebody whose nose is always runny, who likes to collect useless garbage, and who has a habit of saying 'Really?' all the time."

"Really?"

"Really. My most precious possession."

"Does all that mean me?"

"Yes. That's right."

She rubbed her cheek against his.

"I want you to grow up to be a wonderful person."

She kissed his cheek, brushed his hair back, and kissed his forehead.

"I won't be able to be here to see you, but I will always be hoping for you, that your life will be full of love."

"Will you be on Archive?"

"That's where I'll be. On Archive, I will always be thinking of you."

"I will never forget you," Yuji whispered, clinging to his mother's neck. "I will always remember you, so that when the time comes for Takkun to go to Archive he will be able to meet you there."

"Thank you. I will never forget either. My boy. I love you," she said, and hugged him again, hard.

"My life was short, but it was very full, because I had you."

Thank you.

"Look after your dad for me. Try to take care of him the way I would."

"Yes, I will."

Mio took her handkerchief and wiped Yuji's tears and his nose.

"I won't be leaving right away," she said. "Don't worry."

Yuji nodded, and the two of them joined hands and set off again.

The forest ended, and the sky cleared.

Yuji became intent on hunting for treasures. His treasures all had screw threads, or little teeth, or other things like that.

It threatened to rain.

She swept her wet hair from her face with both hands, revealing the beautifully shaped forehead I had known since we were both fifteen. A few strands of her black hair still stuck to her forehead.

"Was that okay?" she asked.

"Yeah. Hearing it from you, Yuji was finally able to forgive himself."

"He was suffering so much."

"I'm to blame for not noticing. I should have listened better."

"It's not your fault either," she said breezily. "It goes without saying, but I'll say it anyway." Like that.

I nodded. My heart felt lighter.

We stood with our backs to the crumbling wall. Right behind us was the door with the number five painted on it. Next to us was the mailbox on its bent post. Everything was wet with rain, which made it look even older than it really was.

"Takkun," Mio said.

"Hmm?"

Her voice seemed the same as usual, so I responded in the usual way.

"I think I'll be going soon," she said. As casually as if she were saying "I'll see you again this evening."

But that was not to be.

She held out her right hand for me to see. From the second joint forward, her fingertips had disappeared, leaving only a faint outline. What had been there seemed to have gone to some other place. The fingers that should have been there were transparent. I could see the forest right through them.

In my heart, I heard the sound of the switch flipping: *Click!*

The valves opened wide, and the gauge maxed out.

"Does it hurt?" I asked, my voice trembling with anxiety.

With a strange expression on her face, she was staring at her fingers (or at the space where her fingers should have been).

"It doesn't hurt. But my fingertips feel cold."

"So…you still have them then?"

"Yes. I'm sure. Somewhere."

"Are you going there now?"

"I think that's what's happening."

"What should I do?"

"Hold my hand," she said with a lonely smile. "Please. Until the very end."

"I understand."

With my right hand I held Mio's left hand. Hard.

As if I believed that could help me hold her here on this earth.

Her slender fingers squeezed my hand in return.

Her fingers were trembling faintly. She was afraid. I could sense a strong anxiety. Even so, she was trying to maintain an outward calm, for my sake.

"Be strong," I told myself.

For her.

"Don't worry," I said. "I'm right here."

Mio nodded, but her face had turned pale.

Our hands entwined, our hearts as one, we got past the first storm of anxiety.

For a second, calm ensued.


"Takkun," she said. "Take care of Yuji for me."

"Yeah."

"Love him enough for me too."

"Yeah."

Before long, though, her words were broken off. She tilted her head and bit her lip. Her big eyeteeth peered out from behind her thin lips.

She closed her eyes, and a line of tears fell.

"This is hard," she said. "I don't want to leave. I want to

stay here. I want to see Yuji grow up. I want to stay beside you forever."

She exhaled, and lifted her face.

"I have to stop. If I keep saying things like this, it will just make it harder for you."

"It's okay. Tell me everything you're really thinking."

She closed her eyes again and nodded slightly.

"No. I can't. You say something. Tell me a story."

"I…" The words that came to my lips were the words I had always in my heart. "…Only wanted to make you happy."

I squeezed her hand. She squeezed back.

"I wanted to take you to see a movie. I wanted to look out at the night, the two of us, from the top of a tall building. Drinking wine or something. Like any ordinary couple. I wanted everything to be normal."

But I couldn't.

Mio's short life ended in this tiny town. No matter how much she might have been able to venture into the wide world, she stayed close to her husband, never leaving this place, living a life of shepherding small joys that others might view as insignificant.

Like self-portraits collected in inexpensive frames. Those kinds of small joys.

"I'm so sorry," I said.

She turned to me with moist eyes and a stiff smile. "Why?" she said, her voice nasal with tears. "Why is it that the men in this family are always apologizing?"

Her thin lips had lost all color, and they trembled faintly.

"I am happy. I do not need anything. All I want is to be next to you. That is the greatest happiness in this world."

"Really?"

"Yeah," she said. "Be confident. You're a wonderful person."

"Only you would say that."

234

"That's not true."

"It is so. You're not like other people. You should have better taste."

She said nothing, but gazed at me kindly, quietly.

"Takkun, have I made you happy?"

"I am happy. More than happy. Just the fact that you married me made me happier than I deserve."

"Really?"

"Yeah."

Mio's arms were now gone, to above the elbow. We had only a little time left.

"Take care of yourself," she said.

Her big eyes filled with tears, and the rims were bright pink.

"That's all I'm worried about."

"I will. I'll try to get at least a little better."

"Do your best! Live!"

"Yeah."

"Your burdens are just a little heavier than most people's. With just a little effort, you can go as far as you want."

"Yeah. I can."

Her form suddenly flickered. The sensation of our entwined fingers became fainter. The lower half of her body was no longer visible.

Even at that, she was still trying to tell me things.

"I feel so comfortable next to you...If I could, I would always want to stay beside you."

"Yeah."

"I love you. I love you so much. I'm so happy to have been your wife."

"Me too. Me too..."

She gave a big smile.

Or half a smile.

"Thank you. Takkun."

Someday, somewhere, may we meet again.

Words floated up, nowhere.

I looked at my hand. All that was left of her was a pink mist. Before long, the breeze would take even that away.

But her scent lingered.

That scent.

The most intimate message she ever transmitted to me.

The only message in the world.

"Mio," she said. "Is that my name?"

"Yes, it is."

That's your name.

That is the name of my wife, the one and only woman in the world I have ever loved, from the very bottom of my heart.

Goodbye, Mio.

Yuji came running up, out of breath.

"Look!"

In his upheld hand he had a sprocket.

"Isn't it great? I'm going to give it to Mom. Where is Mom?"

I couldn't bring myself to say it. I just nodded over and over, smiling stiffly, holding back my tears.

"Where is she? Tell me."

As I stood there, close-mouthed, he ran away again.

"Mom? Where are you?"

"Look, I found something great! I want to give it to you!"

"Where are you, Mom?"

Mom?

Mom?

# 26.

It was two days after Mio left that the rainy season official-ly ended. She must have been in a terrible hurry to start her journey.

And so Yuji and I resumed life on our own.

Even at that though, in all corners of the apartment lingered memories of her. Memories of a woman who had been with us for only six weeks.

"Are you?" she had asked.

"Are you happy? Have I made you happy?"

Each time I remembered those words, I called out to her on her far distant planet.

"You always asked that, didn't you? If you were making me happy? Maybe you never realized, but simply that my wife thinks of me that way is happiness itself."

Another thing you always said was, "You did your best. You're great."

If I thought I would never hear that again it would make me very sad. It was only because you encouraged me that I had any courage at all. I could have taken a rocket to Pluto. If I said that, though, you would have winked exaggeratedly, repeatedly, and made a face that told me to quit lying.

Yuji and I were on our own again, but we were doing much better than before. Yuji had become a much more reliable partner, even a little bit of a grown-up.

In the past he had always slept in his Banzai! posture, but recently he had learned to sleep face down, as if saluting. His right elbow is lifted high, fingertips at his temple. It looks painful, but he seems to be sleeping peacefully. I wonder who he is saluting all night long in his sleep?

When he wakes up in the morning, he says "Good morning" to the photograph on top of the armoire. The photo of us we took at the botanical garden. Mio and I stand next to one another, smiling, with Yuji between us. With the white flowers of the crape myrtle tree behind us, we all look very happy. The expressions on our faces suggest we are people who see a big, beautiful, unknown world spreading out before us.

After that, Yuji waters his Kaguyahime plant and helps take out the trash.

We put on fresh clothes every day. At mealtimes, we eat neatly, not spilling things. When we hang the laundry out to dry, we don't forget to beat the wash, just the way Mio taught us.

In the evening, I practice calligraphy and write the next portion of the book. Before we go to sleep, I read *Jim Button* to Yuji. On weekends we go to the forest, and Yuji looks for bolts at the ruined factory.

Every day I ride my bicycle to work where, as always, I check the notes I have written to myself to make sure I am getting my work done. Ms. Nagase no longer behaves oddly. I have learned to wear suits that are appropriate for the season. I also get my hair cut once a month. And my boss still naps at his desk.

Every day he looks more and more like a St. Bernard.

In this way, little by little, we drifted to a place far away from that day.

Even so, Mio was still with us. Beside me, beside Yuji, she was there.

When I practice calligraphy, I feel like she is looking over my shoulder. I can smell her scent, I even feel as if I can hear her voice.

"Takkun."

I feel as if she is calling me, and every time I turn around to answer her.

When we lie down to sleep, I can feel her warmth beside me. I have a ticklish feeling on my neck, and I hear her voice giggling as she asks, "Best position?"

Before long, the sounds of autumn arrived.

The insects of autumn, the soft rustling of the ripening rice in the paddies. Our Kaguyahime produced some magnificent, sweet-smelling yellow flowers.

"This is Mom," Yuji said. "It even smells like her."

"You're right."

She was right beside us, always.

## 27.

Beneath a clear and balmy sky that stretched on forever, we headed for the train station on our bicycles. We were going to see Nombre, at his new home, in a town by the edge of the sea, a two-hour train ride away.

Mio had wanted us to do this. She was always worried about him.

"Don't you think he's lonely, all by himself?"

"He must be needing something."

She had wanted to go visit him on her own, but his condition prevented it, and in the end it was left undone.

Before she left, she asked me to go, as a favor to her. I wanted to see him myself. There was a lot I wanted to talk to him about: Mio, Pooh, the book.

And so, what happened was, I decided to go. At the moment I made that decision, however, my heart rate increased by twenty beats per minute.

Fantastic.

The Pluto astronaut's depression. That's how I felt.

When we arrived at the station, the first thing that surprised me was the automatic ticket vending machines. In the last ten years I had not been a regular visitor to train stations and these machines had evolved rapidly. They had about twice as many buttons as before, LCD displays, and complicated procedures for purchasing children's tickets. The tickets that came out were flimsy, like something from a child's game. Apparently you're supposed to insert them in a slot in the automatic gate.

I knew about automatic gates from watching TV. Even so, I experienced an inordinate tension as I approached the gate, worse than anything I had suffered since my last encounter with a revolving door at some hotel.

Somehow or other I got through it. By that point, I was already pretty exhausted.

I said to Yuji, "Let's take a local line."

"The express will be faster."

"Yeah, but I don't want to take the express. Too long between stops."

"What happens if it's long?"

"Nothing. But if something did happen, I would be upset."

"Really?"

"Really."

On the local, we would make over forty stops.

Run…stop, with a long sighing exhale of breath, "Haaaah…" and then the train would slowly gather speed again. Forty times.

Eventually the train came, and we boarded.

My legs trembled. I held Yuji's hand tight.

"Takkun," he said.

"What?"

"Your hand is really sweaty." A cold sweat, of course.

The door closed, and at the moment the train started to move, I could hear the sound: *Click!* That old familiar sound. Between my heart and my stomach.

I pulled out my tinted bottle of sandalwood oil and used the dropper to put a drop on a handkerchief, and held it to my mouth. The sweet smell spread through my sinuses. The valve inside me still opened, but the release of the chemicals was held to a minimum.

I was standing right by the door, concentrating on the landscape outside the window.

"Let's sit down. The train is practically empty."

"Thanks, but I prefer to stand."

"Really?"

"Yeah. It makes me feel better."

"Wow. This is really hard for you."

I decided to count the cars on the road that paralleled the tracks. Anything to distract me from the fact that I was on a train.

"One...two...three...four..."

"What is it?"

"I'm counting cars."

"Wow, that sounds like fun. Me too."

"Fine with me."

This became our game. I decided to pretend it was not a way of forgetting we were on a train, it was a game. In the end, though, all this meant was that I kept repeating in my head, "This is a game." No way a game like that is any fun.

Before long, there were only fields, and no more cars to count. And as the number of cars diminished, the chemicals flourished in inverse proportion. I held my hands to my chest to check my heart rate. I gulped in big breaths, and let them out slowly.

I pursed my lips, and made "po, po, po" sounds.

"Po, po, po, po, po."

"What are you doing?"

Po?

"What is that?"

"Saying po, po, po like this is helping me to calm down."

"Really?"

"You do it too."

"Po, po, po, po, po."

"Po, po, po, po, po."

"Takkun," Yuji said. "Everybody's looking at us."

"They just can't keep their eyes off you 'cause you're so cute."

"That's not true."

"Hmm."

"We should sing!"

"Sing?"

"Yeah, you know. Mom's song. The song Mom taught us."

"That's right! That song!"

"Shall we sing it together?"

"Yeah. Let's sing."

"Quietly, okay? Your voice is really loud."

"Okay."

*One elephant began to play*
*Upon a spider's web one day,*
*He found it such tremendous fun*
*That he called for another elephant to come.*

Somehow or other, this was how I got through it. Sniffing sandalwood, counting cars, making po-po-po sounds, and singing with Yuji. Along the way, I had to get off the train three times and wait for several other trains to pass before I was relaxed enough to get back on. Yuji never complained, and he kept me good company.

As I had imagined, it was a long way to Pluto.

"Haaaah…"

The facility was on a mountain overlooking the sea. It was a simple, clean-looking, six-story building. I asked at the reception desk where we might find Nombre's room. He was on the third floor, at the end of the hall. We went up the stairs, heading for the third floor.

"There is an elevator."

"I know. But I prefer to take the stairs."

"Why?"

"Because you never know where an elevator is going to take you."

"Really?"

"I mean, it's got no windows, and the doors slam shut, and you don't know where it's taking you. Maybe to Mars."

"Really?"

"Really. The world's worst method of transportation."

"You're strange."

Nombre was in his room, sitting up in bed and reading a book. He was alone.

"Hello."

At the sound of my voice, he looked up from his book.

"Oh!" he practically shouted, and he gave a big nod. "You came to see me!"

"Yes, we did," Yuji said.

Nombre set his book on the bedside table, rotated on his bottom and put his feet on the floor.

"Let's go to the roof," he said. "It's great up there. The view is wonderful."

Nombre got to his feet slowly, cautiously. He grabbed the cane that stood beside the bed.

"Okay, let's go."

His left leg dragged a little, but he led the way.

"All thanks to rehabilitation," he said, looking back at us. "I can walk on my own two legs again."

His color was good, and his voice was steady.

"You do seem to have gotten much better."

"Yes indeed. My old lifestyle was rotten. Here I'm much healthier."

"It seems so."

Nombre and Yuji took the elevator, while I stubbornly elected to take the stairs. As soon as I opened the door to the roof, my entire field of vision was bathed in blues. Nombre and Yuji looked at me and laughed.

"You sure took your time."

"I didn't want to end up on Mars."

"You're strange."

The roof was covered with artificial turf with a few benches. Here and there were groups of old people and their families. Everyone was talking quietly and looking out at the sea.

"What a fantastic view!"

"Don't you think?"

"How many years has it been since I've seen the sea? For Yuji this must be the first time ever."

"The real thing."

"Yes, this is the real thing."

"It's kinda scary."

"Yeah. That's what's so great about the real thing."

The blue sky had that faint pattern of cirrocumulus clouds called a mackerel sky. Like a flock of birds migrating south, the clouds seemed to be heading for somewhere beyond the horizon.

A cool sea breeze fluttered Yuji's honey-colored hair.

"Did Mio go?"

I nodded at Nombre's words. I had already written him a letter telling the outline of the story.

"Somehow, the whole story seemed to be over before we knew it."

"She came with the rains, and with the rains she left..."

A person like hydrangeas, Nombre muttered.

"But the truth is, I fell in love with her all over again."

Mmm-hmm, Nombre nodded.

"It was a love that lasted just six weeks, but it made me very happy."

Nombre looked up at the mackerel clouds high in the sky.

"Aio," he said.

"Yes?"

"How many people in this world do you think have been lucky enough to have an encounter such as yours?"

Slowly he lowered his gaze, looked at me, and smiled. Deep in his teary eyes, his pale pupils radiated a gentle light.

"As many times as I meet her, I will be lured to her. Over and over."

His trembling finger pointed to the horizon.

"That's right. The sky and the sea inevitably meet and become one. Everywhere. Always."

Each and every one of us always continues to look for that one and only partner.

*"Is anybody there? Looking for a partner in love."*

"You two actually found each other."

"It seems we did."

"Just like the sea."

"Just like the sky?"

I also told Nombre the details of the end of the story of Pooh.

"Ah, that dog always was a free spirit," he said, after hearing me out to the end. "I bet he just couldn't stand being tied up like that."

"Do you think he's still alive?"

"Oh, sure. He's a strong dog. I'm sure he's doing just as he pleases somewhere."

*Hew-wick*? Yuji mimicked repeatedly, looking clever.

"Did you know?" he said. "Pooh could howl. Just like this!" Hew-wick?

Yuji was a good mimic, and he reproduced Pooh's howl perfectly. I couldn't possibly have done it. It was falsetto, but not just that: it was a strange sound such as a person being strangled might make.

"A sound like that?" Nombre asked.

"Yeah. He howled."

"When we left your old house, that was the first time I ever heard him howl like that."

"I never knew," Nombre said. "He was quite a faker. Putting on that he couldn't bark like that. I'm impressed."

"He seemed lonely. He missed you, and he didn't want to leave the house."

"I'm the same way. I miss him too."

"But..." Nombre continued. "Life goes on. No matter how many meetings and partings we have to live through, no matter what faraway places we are sent off to, life goes on."

"Well, it's gotten chilly. Shall we go in?"

Back in the room, Nombre opened the drawer of the table, and pulled out a white envelope.

"This is for you," he said.

I took it from him. On the back was written *Mio Aio*.

"Mio gave me that three days before she went into the hospital," Nombre said. "She handed it to me in the park, and asked

247

me to give it to you in one year, after the rainy season ended."

Nombre sat down on the bed and put aside his cane.

"I don't know what it says. Mio never told me. I was worried about it, though, and I am relieved that I have been able to give it to you."

I looked it over carefully, and then put it in the breast pocket of my jacket.

"Thank you so much. Thanks for keeping it for me all this time."

"It's all right. I was worried, though. I was thinking I might die before I had a chance to give it to you."

"That would never..."

"Oh, it might have. At any rate, with this my work is done."

"What could it be though? And why now?"

"When she gave it to me she had this look, as if she could see something in the future. I think she knew something then that she wanted the you of today to read."

"You may be right."

When the time came for us to leave, we stood up.

"We'll be back."

"Please do come again. It made me so happy to see you. It will give me something to look forward to, to know that you're coming again."

"Of course we will." I said it again, pressing both hands to my chest.

"Well then..."

"Forgive me if I don't see you to the entrance."

"It's all right."

We backed away from Nombre's bed and turned in the middle of the room to head for the door. Leaving the room, we looked back at Nombre, who was still watching us.

"Bye-bye," Yuji said, and Nombre waved a shaky hand.

*Takkun,* she addressed me.

*Takkun, how are you? How is your health?*

In the train on the way home, holding tight to the hand strap, I stood by the door and read the letter from Mio. Yuji counted the cars on the road that paralleled the tracks.

*Takkun, how are you?*

*How is your health?*

*In three days I will be going into the hospital, and I have decided to write you this letter while I still have some freedom to move about.*

*Right now, you are at work. In about an hour, Yuji will come home from kindergarten. If I finish this letter, I plan to give it to Nombre on my way home from grocery shopping for supper.*

*I will ask him to give it to you in one year, after the rainy season has ended.*

*I know that by then I will not be beside you.*

*Has my ghost already gone back to Archive?*

*Are you surprised I know about that?*

*Did you know I could see the future?*

*Actually, I can't.*

*It's a joke.*

*Even a serious, model student like me can tell a joke sometimes.*

*What I am about to write, though, is the truth.*

*This truth may surprise you even more. But it is the unvarnished truth. It is something that actually happened to me.*

*For you to understand the whole thing, I will have to start the story back when we were twenty.*

*Okay?*

*Please read the whole thing.*

*First, the letter from you.*

*Come to think of it, that may have been the last letter I ever got from you. Unforeseeable circumstances kept you from writing again. "Goodbye," you wrote to me, in black ballpoint.*

*Three lines.*

*That was it? The end of our relationship?*

*Unforeseeable circumstances? What was that supposed to mean?*

*I read that brief letter over and over again. And each time I cried.*

*All I could think of to do was to keep writing to you. I bit back the questions that rose to my tongue, pretended not to notice you were breaking it off, and I kept on writing and sending to you little notes about my mundane life.*

*It was a lonely task, like being called to some far-off planet.*

*Reading what I wrote, you would probably smile as if at some dream, and say, "Is that so?" And I would think of your smile, and smile with you.*

*And then, unable to stand the pain anymore, on that day I went to see you at the convenience store where you worked.*

*That took all the courage I had.*

*What you said to me was: "It will be nice if we meet again someday." And then you added: "At our weddings."*

*Do you remember?*

*I felt as if the earth had opened beneath my feet.*

*I knew that you were trying to use those cold words to push me away from you.*

*But you didn't seem to know it yourself.*

*I am a tougher person than you give me credit for, and I can only think about things in practical terms. If I really like somebody, it is not easy for me to just forget about them or suddenly start hating them. God made me to have just one love in my life. And so I went* on, living day by day, thinking of you.

There must have been a reason.

That is what I thought, as I held tightly to a slender thread of hope.

A year passed, and then my "fateful day" arrived.

It was a rainy day in June.

I was riding home from work on my bicycle, and on the country road near my house I was hit by a car. It was not a serious accident. I fell off the bike, but I had no visible injuries.

I got up right away and took a few steps. But then I fainted.

The flow and order of my thoughts at that time are difficult to write about exactly. So let me write about what I surmised later must have happened.

That takes us to our next scene.

When I came to, it was raining, and I was squatting by the ruins of a factory.

Do you see?

That is the secret I have kept from you all this time.

When I was twenty-one years old, I was hit by a car and knocked eight years into the future.

Jump.

I always was good at that.

Even so, that was a big jump.

For you, reading this letter now, I am describing the events of just a short while ago.

Remember my headache? It was because I had hit my head in the car accident. A doctor later found a small hemorrhage in my brain. I think that's also why I completely lost my memory.

This is what I think, though.

*I think the human heart was not made to go outside its time. If people temporarily lose their memory it must be some way of protecting their sanity. I mean, if I had had my memory, I would have been very confused.*

*When I returned to my own time, I lost my memory again. I forgot all about the six weeks I had spent with you and Yuji. It was only two months later that I fully recovered that memory.*

*Another theory might be that the "Somebody" who created our world by joking around with that little jump in time, also made me lose my memory as a way of showing he cared about me.*

*Sitting here now, writing, remembering that time, I cannot help but be aware of the existence of a "Will" that tries to reel in human fate. Those six weeks I spent with you were to change the rest of my life.*

*It was by no means a coincidence that the twenty-one-year-old me jumped to that specific place and time. I had prayed for a whole year to understand what was going on with you, the reasons behind your words, and "Somebody" took pity on me and reached out his hand.*

*I still think that.*

*Even so, you two were quite a mess when I met you, weren't you? You and Yuji, living in that filthy apartment, littered with stuff. Wearing clothes stained with food, badly in need of haircuts. Yuji with a whole year's worth of wax in his ears. I get worried thinking that is the phase of your life you are about to enter.*

*But everything is going to be okay. You'll straighten out. Even without me, you will have each other, and you will have a good life.*

*I do believe it.*

*At that time, your seizure came as quite a shock to me. By now I've gotten used to them, but that one was the first I ever witnessed. I had told you not to take that antipyretic, but you must have forgotten, didn't you? They say you can't change history. Is that why?*

*With this confession, now you also understand why my eyeglass prescription wasn't right, and why I had no sexual experience.*

*Still, it is a strange story, isn't it?*

*The twenty-one-year-old me losing my virginity to the twenty-nine-year-old you. And two months later doing it all over again.*

*That time you thought was the first time for both of us, but that wasn't quite true.*

*That's why it was so easy for us to become as one that time.*

*What do you think of this?*

*Have I hurt you?*

*I think this was all ideal. You're sure to say I'm thinking too pragmatically though.*

*Those six weeks were over in an instant.*

*I was very happy.*

*I fell in love with you, and I heard from you a fantastic love story, and I realized the joy of knowing that we were the stars of the story.*

*And I got to know Yuji.*

*My very own boy.*

*The English prince.*

*The elementary school Yuji was just a little bit sturdier than my boy is right now.*

*They grow up so fast.*

*I'm sure he'll make a wonderful grown-up someday.*

*I'm looking forward to it.*

*A few more facts that I learned.*

*My own fate, written in your book.*

*That I leave this world at age twenty-eight.*

*And that I was a ghost!*

*Of course, that was your mistake. But at that time, you had me believing it myself.*

*I had a constant sense of unreality, that I was somehow in suspension. Your behavior, the two of you, was so unnatural. When we would go out, I often sensed wonderment in your gaze. That was all because you thought I was a ghost.*

*I believed it myself, and never doubted it.*

*So then, when it came time for us to part again, that was really hard. I honestly thought I would be going to Archive. It made me lonely to think I was leaving you. I was frightened at the thought of leaving this world.*

*I will never forget Yuji crying as he hurled those angry words at me.*

*Sitting here now, thinking of the pain he will have to suffer, my own heart hurts for him. Someday, when he gets even bigger, I want you to tell him what I really thought of him. I want you to tell him what I have written in this letter. I hope that will help him be strong and take life as it comes.*

*I will go on.*

*After I left the two of you at that place, I returned to my own time. When I came to, I was lying in a hospital bed. Only a few hours had passed since the accident. I had jumped eight years into the future and come straight back to where I was before. My absence was a matter of a fraction of a second.*

*The man who had been driving the car that hit me didn't even seem to notice anything strange.*

*But I had lost my memory.*

*Including the memory of the six weeks I had spent with you two. I didn't know who I was. I spent days just staring vacantly up at the ceiling in the hospital, watching the time go by.*

*After more than a month, my memory slowly started to return.*

*At first I thought my memory of that time was some fantasy I had made up in my head.*

*What a wonderful fantasy it was though.*

*I was uncontrollably attracted to that six weeks I had spent with you.*

*Your kiss.*

*Our walks in the woods.*

*The beautiful boy you said was my own son.*

*The rapid beating of my heart when we made love.*

*But the most important sensation I had was that each and every part of these memories might be true, and had a powerful effect on my emotions.*

*Had that joy been real?*

*The sadness and anxiety of saying goodbye. The sadness in your eyes as you said, "I only wanted to make you happy."*

*In my heart I visited and revisited those days many times, and I came to the conclusion it was definitely real, that I had jumped eight years into the future and come back. And so, the very first thing I did when I was well enough to leave the hospital and go home was to call your house.*

*Your mother said to me, "Takumi is taking a trip."*

*Just as you had said in your book.*

*This confirmed my own conclusions, and I left a message with your mother.*

*"There is something I want to talk about. Please call. I will wait for you forever."*

*After that I sat right in front of the telephone and waited.*

*I knew you would call. I knew we would meet in the town by the lake.*

*And then, the phone rang.*
*I picked up the receiver after the first ring.*
*I couldn't hear a thing, but I knew it would be you.*
*And so, without hesitating, I said, "Aio?"*
*Your voice was shaky.*
*And that's why I said, "Don't worry. It'll be fine."*

*In that town by the lake, when we stopped under the pedestrian bridge, again I told you, "It'll be fine." I knew these words would convince you to decide to marry me.*

*Later, when you asked me, I said I didn't remember, but that was a lie. The truth is, I remembered.*

*The truth is, those words had been my proposal to you.*

*There were many people I looked forward to meeting again in the days to come.*

*I was able to meet Nombre again. He didn't look much different than he would eight years later. Pooh was younger and more energetic. His real name was Alex, I learned when we met again.*

*Yuji was born, and the days passed peacefully.*

*By this time, those six weeks seemed to be far away.*

*My memory of them was hazy, and again at times I began to think they had been a fantasy. At other times I thought it might be a kind of déjà vu.*

*Perhaps I could go beyond the wall of my twenty-eighth year.*

*Without your knowledge, I started taking herbal medicines, to help my body.*

*Even so...*

*The time has come.*

*It seems we cannot escape the fate that has been determined for us.*

*I think you will also understand the reason why I never told you all of this.*

*I did not want you to know that a painful future awaited you. I wanted us to live like any ordinary couple, smiling, with hope for the future.*

*Another thing I thought was: if you knew that a story of happiness you told me yourself had made me decide to call you that day, what would you have thought?*

*What would you do?*

*You might have tried to convince me, the person who arrived eight years earlier, not to marry you. You might have told me some made-up story so that I would go back to my own time wanting to keep my distance from you. But seven years after that day when we met again in that town by the lake, I am sitting here writing this letter to you, and in three weeks I will leave this earth.*

*No matter how much you deny it, you might still think that our marriage had something to do with the reason my life is about to end. Or you might have decided not to have a child.*

*Isn't that right?*

*When I think about these things, though, I get very confused and I can't sort things out. If you had lied to me, and I had given up on the idea of marrying you, then I couldn't be here right now writing this letter. But I certainly did marry you, and we had Yuji. But what would happen if when you come home from work tonight I were to show you this letter?*

*Would we both suddenly disappear?*

*If we had lived separate lives, would that mean Yuji would never have been born?*

*It is all too strange, and more than I can sort out in my head.*

*And so, I will simply keep my secret until I have to go.*

*I would hate it if I had never been with you.*

*I would hate my life without Yuji.*

*What if I had never gone to that town on the lake?*

*I have also toyed with this thought many times.*

*Even that very day, in the train on the way there, I thought about it.*

*I could have gotten out at any station along the way, turned around and gone home. If I hadn't met you that day, what would my life have been like?*

*Would I have married someone else?*

*Would I have lived with that person to a ripe old age?*

*Quiet, peaceful, sufficiently happy days might have awaited me.*

*By the time I became a grandmother, though, I might have thought: Was this the life I wanted to choose? Did I want this life so badly I gave up something important for it?*

*The future rainy season where the twenty-one-year-old me arrives.*

*The childish husband whose expression is so anxious when I'm not there.*

*And my very own English prince.*

*The time I was supposed to spend with them would be lost forever.*

*I would definitely regret that.*

*I know the answer for sure.*

*I had already met the two of you.*

*With that memory in my heart, I could never have lived a different life.*

*I wanted to marry you and have Yuji.*

*I wanted to accompany you and our son in this world.*

*And I wanted to leave this world smiling, with a heart full of happy memories.*

*I made up my mind. I would not get off the train halfway. I would take it to my destination, where I would meet you.*

*I want to go on living.*
*Sometimes I am so afraid of what is about to happen to my body that I just don't know what to do.*
*I truly regret that I won't be here to watch Yuji grow into a fine young man.*
*But this is the life I chose.*
*And so...*

*Soon it will be time for Yuji to come home from school.*
*I have to go meet him. Then I have to go grocery shopping and fix dinner for the two of you. Tonight we'll have Yuji's favorite: curry.*

*I will only be able to make a meal for the two of you a few more times. I wish I could be here for many, many more mealtimes together.*
*I'm sorry.*
*I won't be able to.*

*I will end this letter here.*
*No matter how much I wrote, I would not be able to say all I have to say to you.*
*The fourteen years I have spent with you have been fun. I don't care that we were never able to take a trip together, never able to look out at the nighttime view from atop a tall building together. I have been happy just to be beside you.*
*I will be going on ahead of you, to Archive.*
*Someday, let's meet again there.*
*I will make sure there's a place for you right beside me.*

*Take care of yourself.*
*And take care of Yuji for me.*

*Thank you so much. Really.*
*I love you.*
*From my heart.*

*Goodbye.*
*Mio*


In the envelope was a page torn from a diary.
It was dated August 15.

*It's time.*
*I have to go.*
*At the station by the lake, he's waiting for me, I'm sure.*
*With my wonderful future.*
*Wait for me, will you, my boys?*

*Now, I'm coming to be with you.*

# Epilogue

Today we went to the forest again.
Yuji rode his bicycle, and his shirt was sparkling white.
His hair was neatly cut, and it billowed in the breeze.

We're doing great, don't you think?
Little by little, we're trying to become what you wanted us
to be.
Little by little.
Little by little.
*Poco poco.*

The life you left, I am trying to nurture.
We miss you.

As the final chapter in this little book, that is what I will write.

I run in the woods for about forty minutes.

I am wearing my faded shorts and my KSC T-shirt.

Yuji is riding behind me on his kid's bike.

He doesn't slow me down anymore. Now he can ride that bike like he was born on it.

Emerging from the woods, we arrive at the old factory site.

Yuji hunts for bolts and nuts and coil springs.

I sit down, some distance from him, and doze off a little.

But I know.

He has a secret in his pocket. A letter to send to you, on Archive.

In his childish handwriting (unfortunately, he takes after me), it is addressed to *Ms. Mio Aio, Archive.*

On the back it says, *Yuji Aio.*

When I'm not looking, he slips it into the bent mail slot on the post by door No. 5. (At least he thinks it's a mailbox.)

For some reason, he wants to keep this a secret from me. And so, later, when he is again intent on his treasure hunt, I collect the letters from the slot, being careful that he doesn't see me doing it.

I have never opened them or read them. I collect them, and keep them in the shoebox in the closet.

The next time we come here, he checks to make sure that his last letter has been collected, and he nods. (I am really watching him closely, just pretending to sleep.)

And that is how he continues his story to you, on Archive.

On rainy weekends, Yuji is particularly anxious to visit the old factory site. So we take our umbrellas, and we walk.

I spread a plastic sheet on the old machinery platform and sit down. Yuji pretends to look for bolts, and slowly makes his approach to door No. 5.

And there, in a quiet voice, he calls to you.

Mom?

Yuji is a believer.

He believes that someday, you will walk right through door No. 5 and come back to us.

He is sure it will be a rainy day when that happens.

My English prince, with his golden hair, is calling out for you again today.

Mom?

Mom?

Mom?

# Afterword

*Be With You* is an autobiographical book. Many writers seem to want to deny the autobiographical elements of their fictional works, but I do not generally share this way of thinking. All I hope to do is to tell things well.

When my book became a million-seller in Japan, most of the questions that came to me focused on two main points:

"Which parts of this book are true?" and,

"What are your thoughts on true love?"

In response to the first question, I usually replied, "The things that appear to be normal are fiction; the things that appear to be impossible or imaginary are true." (Of course my wife did not come back as a ghost. Even now she is happy and healthy.) Life itself can sometimes seem that way. It might seem impossible or imaginary that a forty-year-old man who has always felt himself to be on the outer perimeter of ordinary society might write a book about the love between himself and his wife, and that that book might become a best-seller and be translated into a lot of different languages and be read all over the world. Or it might seem impossible or imaginary that a pencil, stuck and forgotten in the pages of a book that was returned, might lead to the re-connection of two people whose relationship had been on the verge of fading away.

My relationship with my mother and my relationship with my wife form the basis of this book. My mother risked her life to bring a son into this world. The birth ultimately caused her health to fail and greatly changed her life after that point. How should I, who am that son, deal with that? Or how about my wife, who made up her mind to spend her life with a man like me, a man who embraces so many faults? Given these facts, the book I wrote was practically automatic.

By sheer coincidence, just as my book was published, Japan was in the throes of a "Pure Love" boom, and I was swept up in the middle of this movement. Because I was well aware that I was far from being a typical person, and that my wife, as someone who could bring herself to love someone like me, must be pretty out of the ordinary herself, the idea that our relationship could be seen as some sort of ideal form of the love between normal people caused me considerable consternation. I have said a lot of different things in response to the public, but what I was really thinking was, "This is not something that came about because I desired it."

When it comes to personality, I am definitely a minority. I think in every society there must be people like me who have trouble controlling their hearts. These are the people who may best be able to understand the actions of my main character.

But it was never my intention to write something for just a narrow group of people. My foremost aim was to write something entertaining, something people would be able to read and enjoy.

This book uses the framework of a traditional ghost story to say something about time and memory. There is no evil or violence (in fact it is quite sentimental). For me, though, that is what makes this book so real. I am astonished and delighted that a voice that emerged naturally from my flesh has reached such distant places. At the same time, I now sincerely hope that the true meaning of this book has been well told.

*Takuji Ichikawa*
*April 2006*

# About the Author

Author Takuji Ichikawa was born in Tokyo in 1962 and is a graduate of Dokkyo University. His first novel, *Separation*, was published in 2002. *Be With You* (published in Japan as *Ima, Ai ni Yukimasu* in 2003) is his first work to be translated into English.

## A NOTE ABOUT THE TYPE

Apollo was designed in 1964 by Adrian Frutiger
for the Monotype Corporation. It was the first
typeface family to be commissioned by
Monotype exclusively for phototypesetting and
the emerging litho printing technology.